Bailey wanted to say no. She desperately wanted to throw the offer back in his face and walk out of there, dignity intact.

But two things stopped her. Jared Stone was offering her the one thing she'd sworn she'd never stop working for until she got it. And despite everything else that he was—impossible, arrogant and full of himself—he was brilliant. And everyone knew it. If she worked alongside him as his equal she could write her own ticket. Ensure she never went back to the life she'd vowed to leave behind forever.

Survival was stronger than her pride. It always had been. And men having all the power in her world wasn't anything unusual. She knew how to play them. How to beat them. And she could beat Jared Stone too. She knew it.

She stared at him. At the haughty tilt of his chin. It was almost irresistible to show him how wrong he was. About her. About all women. This would be her gift to the female race…

"All right. On two conditions."

His gaze narrowed.

"Double my salary and give me the title of CMO."

"We don't have a Chief Marketing Officer."

"Now we do."

"Fine."

His curt agreement made her eyes widen, brought her swinging back around.

"You can have both."

S'   deal of
tr   euphoria
d   made a
d   id for it.

Jennifer Hayward has been a fan of romance and adventure since filching her sister's Harlequin Mills & Boon® novels to escape her teenaged angst.

Jennifer penned her first romance at nineteen. When it was rejected, she bristled at her mother's suggestion that she needed more life experience. She went on to complete a journalism degree and intern as a sports broadcaster before settling into a career in public relations. Years of working alongside powerful, charismatic CEOs and traveling the world provided perfect fodder for the arrogant alpha males she loves to write about, and free research on the some of the world's most glamorous locales.

A suitable amount of life experience under her belt, she sat down and conjured up the sexiest, most delicious Italian wine magnate she could imagine, had him make his biggest mistake and gave him a wife on the run. That story, THE DIVORCE PARTY, won her Harlequin's *So You Think You Can Write* contest and a book contract. Turns out Mother knew best!

A native of Canada's gorgeous east coast, Jennifer now lives in Toronto with her Viking husband and their young Viking-in-training. She considers her ten-year-old book club, comprising some of the most amazing women she's ever met, a sacrosanct date in her calendar. And some day they will have their monthly meeting at her fantasy beach house, waves lapping at their feet, wine glasses in hand.

You can find Jennifer on Facebook and Twitter.

Recent titles by the same author:
CHANGING CONSTANTINOU'S GAME
THE TRUTH ABOUT DE CAMPO
AN EXQUISITE CHALLENGE
THE DIVORCE PARTY

THE MAGNATE'S MANIFESTO

BY
JENNIFER HAYWARD

Published in Great Britain 2014
by Mills & Boon, an imprint of Harlequin (UK) Limited,
Eton House, 18-24 Paradise Road, Richmond, Surrey, TW9 1SR

© 2014 Jennifer Drogell

ISBN: 978-0-263-90926-5

Harlequin (UK) Limited's policy is to use papers that are natural, renewable and recyclable products and made from wood grown in sustainable forests. The logging and manufacturing processes conform to the legal environmental regulations of the country of origin.

Printed and bound in Spain
by Blackprint CPI, Barcelona

THE MAGNATE'S MANIFESTO

A big thanks to Rebecca Avalon of *Strip and Grow Rich*, the original stripper school, for taking me inside the life and mind of a dancer and helping me bring Bailey to life. I can't thank you enough!

CHAPTER ONE

THE DAY THAT Jared Stone's manifesto sparked an incident of international female outrage happened to be, unfortunately for Stone, a slow news day. By 5:00 a.m. on Thursday, when the sexy Silicon Valley billionaire was reputed to be running the trails of San Francisco's Golden Gate Park, as he did every morning in his connected-free beginning to the day, his manifesto was dinner conversation in Moscow. In London, as chicly dressed female office workers escaped brick and steel buildings to chase down lunch, his outrageous state of the union on twenty-first-century women was on the tip of every tongue, spoken in hushed, disbelieving tones on elevator trips down to ground level.

And in America, where the outrage was about to hit hardest, women who had spent their entire careers seeking out the C-suite only to find themselves blocked by a glass ceiling that seemed impossible to penetrate stared in disbelief at their smartphones. *Maybe it was a joke*, some said. *Someone must have hacked into Stone's email,* said others. *Doesn't surprise me at all*, interjected a final contingent, many of whom had dated Stone in an elusive quest to pin down the world's most sought-after bachelor. *He's a cold bastard. I'm only surprised his true stripes didn't appear sooner.*

At her desk at 7:00 a.m. at the Stone Industries building in San Jose, Bailey St. John was oblivious to the firestorm her boss was creating. Intent on hacking her way through her own glass ceiling and armed with a steaming Americano with which to do so, she slid into her chair with as much grace as her pencil skirt would allow, harnessed a morning dose of optimism that today would be different, and flicked on her PC.

She stared sleepily at the screen as her computer booted up. Took a sip of the strong, acrid brew that inevitably kicked her brain into working order as she clicked on her mail program. Her girlfriend Aria's email, titled "OMG," made her lift a recently plucked and perfected brow.

She clicked it open. The hot sip of coffee she'd just taken lodged somewhere in her windpipe. *Billionaire Playboy Ignites International Incident With His Manifesto on Women*, blared the headline of the variety news site everyone in Silicon Valley frequented. *Leaked Tongue-in-Cheek Manifesto to His Fellow Mates Makes Stone's Views on Women in the Boardroom and Bedroom Blatantly Clear.*

Bailey put down her coffee with a jerky movement and clicked through to the manifesto that had already generated two million views. *The Truth About Women,* which apparently had never been meant for anyone other than Jared Stone's inner circle, was now the salacious entertainment of the entire male population. As she started reading what was unmistakably her boss's bold, eloquent tone, she nearly fell off her chair.

Having dated and worked with a cross-section of women from around the globe, and having reached the age where I feel I can make a definitive opinion on the subject matter, I have come to a conclusion. Women lie.

They say they want to be equals in the boardroom, when in reality nothing has changed over the past fifty years. Despite all their pleas to the contrary, despite their outrage at the limits the "so-called" glass ceiling puts on them, they don't really want to be hammering out a deal, and they don't want to be orchestrating a merger. They want to be home in the house we provide, living the lifestyle to which they've become accustomed. They want a man who will take care of them, who gives them a hot night between the sheets and diamond jewelry at appropriate intervals. Who will prevent them from drifting aimlessly through life without a compass...

Drifting aimlessly through life without a compass? Bailey's cheeks flamed. If there was any way in which her life couldn't be described, it was that. She'd spent the last twelve years putting as much mileage between her and her depressing low-income roots as she could, doing the impossible and obtaining an MBA before working herself up the corporate ladder. First at a smaller Silicon Valley start-up, then for the last three years at Jared Stone's industry darling of a consumer electronics company.

And that was where her rapid progression had stopped. As director of North American sales for Stone Industries, she'd spent the last eighteen months chasing a vice president position Stone seemed determined not to give her. She'd worked harder and more impressively than any of her male colleagues, and it was generally acknowledged the VP job should have been hers. Except Jared Stone didn't seem to think so—he'd given the job to someone else. And that hurt coming from the man she'd been dying to work for—the resident genius of Silicon Valley.

Why didn't he respect her as everyone else did?

Her blood heated to a furious level; bubbled and boiled and threatened to spill over into an expression of uncontrolled rage. *Now she knew why.* Because Jared Stone was a male chauvinist pig. The worst of a Silicon Valley breed.

He was...*horrific.*

She forced a sip of the excessively strong java into her mouth before she lost it completely and slammed the cup back down on her desk. Flicked her gaze back to her computer screen and the "rules" on women Jared had also gifted the male population with.

Rule Number 1—All women are crazy. And by that I mean they think in a completely foreign way from us that might as well come from another planet. You need to find the least crazy one you can live with. If you elect to settle down, which I'm not advocating, mind you.

Rule Number 2—Every woman wants a ring on her finger and the white picket fence. No matter what she says. Not a bad thing for the state of the nuclear family or for you if you're already on that trajectory. But for God's sake know what you're getting yourself into.

Rule Number 3—Every woman wants a lion in the bedroom. She wants to be dominated. She wants you to be in complete control. She doesn't want you to listen to her "needs." So stop making that mistake. Be a man.

Rule Number 4—Every woman starts the day with an agenda. A cause, an item to strike off her list, the inescapable conclusion of a campaign she's been running. It could be a diamond ring, more of your time, your acknowledgment that you will indeed agree to meet her mother... Whatever it is, take it from me, just say yes or say goodbye. And know that saying goodbye might be a whole hell of a lot cheaper in the long run.

Bailey stopped reading for the sake of her blood pressure. Here she'd been worrying that the personality conflict she and Jared shared, which admittedly was intense, was the problem. The thing that had been holding her back. Their desire to rip each other apart every time they stepped foot in a boardroom together was legendary within the company, but that hadn't been it. No—in actual fact, he disrespected *the entire female race.*

She'd never even had a chance.

Three years, she fumed, scowling at her computer screen as she pulled up a blank document. Three years she'd worked for that egocentric jerk, racking up domestic sales of his wildly popular cell phones and computers… For what? It had all been a complete waste of time in a career in which the clock was ticking. A CEO by thirty-five, she'd vowed. Although that vision seemed to be fading fast.…

She pressed her lips together and started typing. *To whom it may concern: I can no longer work in an organization with that pig at the helm. It goes against every guiding principle I've ever had.* She kept going, wrote the letter without holding back, until her blood had cooled and her rage was spent. Then she did a second version she could hand in to HR.

She wasn't working for Jared Stone. For that beautiful, arrogant piece of work. Not one minute longer. No matter how brilliant he was.

Jared Stone was in a whistling kind of mood as he parked in the Stone Industries lot, collected his briefcase and made his way through the sparkling glass doors. A five-mile run through the park, a long hot shower, a power shake and a relatively smooth commute could do that for a man.

He hummed a bad version of a song he'd just heard on the radio as he strode toward the bank of elevators that ran up the center of the elegant, architecturally brilliant building. When life was this good, when he was on top of his game, about to land the contract that would silence all his critics, cement his control of his company, he felt impermeable, impenetrable, *unbeatable,* as if he could leap tall buildings in a single bound, solve all the world's problems, bring about world peace even, if given the material to work with.

A gilded ray of brilliance for all to follow.

He stuck his hand between the closing elevator doors and gained himself admittance on a half-filled car. Greeted the half dozen employees inside with the megawatt smile the press loved to capture and made a mental note of who was putting in the extra effort coming in early. Gerald from finance flashed him a swaggering grin as if they shared an inside joke. Jennifer Thomas, PA to one of the vice presidents, who was normally a sucker for his charm, did a double take at his friendly "good morning" and muttered something unintelligible back. The woman from legal, what *was* her name, turned her back on him.

Strange.

The weird vibe only got worse as the doors opened on the executive floors and he made his way through the still-quiet space to his office. Another PA gave him the oddest look. He looked down. Did he have power shake on the front of his shirt? Toothpaste on his face?

Power shake stains ruled out, he frowned at his fifty-something PA, Mary, as she handed him his messages. "What is *wrong* with everyone today? The sun is shining, sales are up…"

Mary blinked. "You haven't been online, have you?"

"You know my theory on that," he returned patiently. "I spend the first couple hours of my day finding my center. Seven-thirty is soon enough to discover what craziness has befallen the world."

"Right," she muttered. "Well, you might want to leave your Buddhist sojourn by the wayside and plug in quickly before Sam Walters arrives. He'll be here at eleven."

Jared brought his brows together at the mention of the

chairman of the Stone Industries board. "I have nothing scheduled with him."

"You do now," she said. "Jared—I—" She set down her pen and gave him a direct look. "Your *document*, your manifesto, was leaked on the internet last night."

He felt the blood drain from his face. He'd only ever written two manifestos in his life. One when he'd started Stone Industries and put down his vision for the company, and the second, the private joke he'd shared with his closest friends last night after a particularly amusing guys' night out on the town.

It had not been intended for public consumption.

From the look on Mary's face, she was *not* talking about the Stone Industries manifesto.

"What do you mean leaked?" he asked slowly.

She cleared her throat. "The document…the whole document is all over the Net. My mother emailed it to me this morning. She asked what I was doing working for you."

The thought crossed his mind that this was all impossible because his buddies would never do that to him. Not over a joke intended for their eyes only…. *Had someone hacked into his email?*

He looked down at the wad of messages in his hand, his chest tightening. "How bad is it?"

Her lips pursed. "It's everywhere."

Thinking he might finally have taken his penchant for stirring things up too far, he knew it for the truth when his mentor and adviser Sam Walters walked into his office three hours later, Jared's legal and PR teams behind him. The sixty-five-year-old financial genius did not look amused.

Jared waved them into chairs and attempted a pre-emptive strike. "Sam, this is all a huge misunderstanding. We'll put out a statement that it was a joke and it'll be gone by tomorrow."

His vice president of PR, Julie Walcott, lifted a brow. "We're at two million hits and climbing, Jared. Women are threatening to boycott our products. This is not going away."

He leaned back against his desk, the abdomen he'd worked to the breaking point this morning contracting at his appalling lack of judgment in ever putting those words on paper. But one thing he never did was show weakness. Particularly not now when the world wanted to eat him alive. "What do you suggest I do?" he drawled, with his usual swagger. "Beg women for their forgiveness? Get down on my knees and swear I didn't mean it?"

"Yes."

He gave her a disbelieving look. "It was a *joke between friends*. Addressing it gives it credence."

"It's now a joke between you and the entire planet," Julie said matter-of-factly. "Addressing it is the only thing that's going to save you right about now."

The sick feeling in his stomach intensified. Sam crossed his arms over his chest. "This has legal implications, Jared. Human rights implications… And furthermore, as I don't need to remind you, Davide Gagnon's daughter is a charter member of a woman's organization. She will not be amused."

Jared's hands tightened around the wooden lip of his desk. He was well aware of Micheline Gagnon's board memberships. The daughter of the CEO of Europe's largest consumer electronics retailer, Maison Electronique—with whom Stone Industries was pursuing a groundbreaking five-year deal to expand its global presence—was an active social commentator. She would *not* be amused. But really…it had been a *joke*.

He let out a long breath. "Tell me what we need to do."

"We need to issue an apology," Julie said. "Position it as a private joke that was in bad taste. Say that it has nothing to do with your real view of women, which is actually one of the utmost respect."

"I *do* respect women," he interjected. "I just don't think they're always honest with their feelings."

Julie gave him a long look. "When's the last time you put a woman on the executive committee?"

Never. He raked a hand through his hair. "Give me a woman who belongs on it and I'll put her there."

"What about Bailey St. John?" Sam lifted his bushy brows. "You seem to be the only one who thinks she hasn't earned her spot as a VP."

Jared scowled. "Bailey St. John is a special case. She isn't ready. She thinks she was *born* ready, but she isn't."

"You need to make a *gesture,*" Sam underscored, his tone taking on a steely edge. "You are on thin ice right now, Jared." *In all aspects,* his mentor's deeply lined face seemed to suggest. "Give her the job. *Get* her ready."

"It's not the right choice," Jared rejected harshly. "She still needs to mature. She's only twenty-nine, for God's sake. Making her a VP would be like setting a firecracker loose."

Sam lifted his brows again as if to remind him how sparse his support on the board was right now. As if he needed *reminding* that his control of the company he'd built from a tiny start-up into a world player was in jeopardy. *His company.*

"Give her the job, Jared." Sam gave him an even look. "Smooth out her raw edges. Do not blow ten years of hard work on your penchant for self-ignition."

Antagonism burned through him, singeing the tips of his ears. He'd stolen Bailey from a competitor three years ago for her incredibly sharp brain. For the potential he knew she had. And she hadn't disappointed him. He had no doubt he'd one day make her into a VP, but right now, she was the rainbow-colored cookie in the pack. You never knew what you were going to bite into when she walked into a room. And he couldn't have that around him. Not now.

Sam gave him a hard look. "Fine," Jared rasped. He'd figure out a way to work the Bailey equation. "What else?"

"Cultural sensitivity training," his head of legal interjected. "HR is going to set it up."

"That," Jared dismissed in a low voice, "is not happening. Next."

Julie outlined her plan to rescue his reputation. It was solid, what he paid her for, and he agreed with it all, except for the cultural sensitivity training, and ended the meeting.

He had way bigger fish to fry. A board's support to solidify. His own job to save.

He paced to the window as the door closed behind the group, attempting to digest how his perfect morning had turned into the day from hell. At the root of it all, the abrupt end to his "relationship" with his trustworthy 10:00 p.m. of late, Kimberly MacKenna. A logical accountant by trade, she'd sworn to him she wasn't looking for anything permanent. So he'd let his guard down, let her in. Then last Saturday night, she'd plopped herself down on his sofa, declared he was breaking her heart and turned those baby blues on him in a look he'd have sworn he'd never see.

Get serious, Jared, they'd said. He had. By 10:00 a.m. on Monday she'd had his trademark diamond tennis bracelet on her arm and another one had bitten the dust.

He'd been sad and maybe a touch lonely when he'd written that manifesto. But those were the rules. No commitment. His mouth twisted as he pressed his palm against the glass. Maybe he should have given his PR team the official line on his parents' marriage. How his mother had bled his father dry... How she'd turned him into half a man. It would have made him much more sympathetic.

Better yet, he thought, Julie could devote more of her

time to controlling the industry media that wanted to lynch him before he'd even gotten his vision for Stone Industries' next decade off the ground. When you'd parlayed a groundbreaking new personal computer created on your best friend's dorm room floor into the most successful consumer electronics company in America, a NASDAQ gold mine, you didn't expect the naysayers to start calling for the CEO's head as soon as the waters got rough. You expected them to trust your vision, radically different though it might be from the rest of the industry, and assume you had a plan to revolutionize the connected home.

A harsh curse escaped his lips. They would rather tear him down than support him. They were carnivores waiting for the kill. Well, it wasn't going to happen. He was going to go to France, tie up this exclusive partnership with Maison Electronique, cut his competitors off at the knees and deliver this deal signed and sealed to the board at his must-win executive committee meeting in two weeks.

All he had to do was present his marketing vision to Davide Gagnon and secure his buy-in, and it was a done deal.

Spinning away from the window, he stalked to the door and growled a command at Mary to get Bailey St. John in his office *now*. He would promote her all right. But he wasn't a stupid man. He would leave himself a loophole so when she proved herself too inexperienced for the job, he could put things back where they belonged until she *was* ready.

His last call was to his head of IT. Whoever had hacked into his email was going to rue the day they'd crossed him. He promised them that.

Bailey had cooled her heels for fifteen minutes outside Jared Stone's office, resignation in hand, when Mary finally motioned her in. Her ability to appear civil at an all-time low, she pushed the heavy wooden door open and moved into the intensely masculine space. Dominated by a massive marble-manteled fireplace and floor-to-ceiling windows, it was purposefully minimalistic; focused like its owner, who preferred to roam the hallways of Stone Industries and work alongside his engineers instead of sitting at a desk.

He turned as her heels tapped across the Italian marble, and as usual when she was within ten feet of him, her composure seemed to slide a notch or two. She might not pursue his assets like every other female in Silicon Valley, but that didn't mean she could ignore them. The piercing blue gaze he turned on her now was legendary for divesting a woman of her clothes faster than she could say "only if you respect me in the morning." And if that didn't do it for you, then his superbly toned body in the exquisitely tailored suit and his razor-sharp brain would. He supplemented his daily running routine with martial arts, and there was a joke going around the Valley that it was no coincidence his name was Stone. As in All-Night Jared Stone.

Heat filled her cheeks as he waved her into a chair, his finely crafted gold cuff links glinting in the sunlight. She started to sink into the sofa, obeying him like his mindless disciples, before she checked herself and straightened. "I'm not here to socialize, Jared. I'm here to resign."

"Resign?" His usual husky, raspy tone held an incredulous edge.

"Yes, resign." She pushed her shoulders back and walked toward him, refusing to let the balance of power shift in his favor as it always did. When she was a few inches away from him, she stopped and lifted her chin, absorbing the impact of that penetrating blue gaze. "I'm tired of *drifting aimlessly* through this company with you lying to me about where I'm headed."

His gaze darkened. "Oh, come on, Bailey. I would think you of all people could take a joke."

She sank her hands into her hips. "You meant every word of that, Jared. And to think I thought it might be our personality conflict that's been holding me back."

The corner of his mouth lifted, the scar that sliced through his upper lip whitening as skin stretched over bone. "You mean the fact that every time we're in a boardroom together we want to dismantle each other in a slow and painful manner?" His eyes took on a smoky, deadly hue. "That's the kind of thing that gets me out of bed in the morning."

The futility of it all sent her head into an exasperated shake. "I think I've always known what your opinion of women is, but stupid me, I thought you actually respected me."

"I do respect you."

"Then why has everything I've done over the past three years failed to impress you? I was a star at my last company, Jared. You recruited me because of it. Why give Tate Davidson the job I deserved?"

"You weren't ready," he stated matter-of-factly, as much in control as she was out of it.

"In what way?"

"Your maturity levels," he elaborated, looking down his perfect nose at her. "Your knee-jerk reactions. Right now is a good example. You didn't even think this through."

Antagonism lanced through her, setting every limb of her body on fire. "Oh, I thought it through all right. I've had three years to think it through. And forgive me if I don't take the maturity criticism too hard after your childish little stunt this morning. You wanted to make every male in California laugh and slap each other on the back? Well, you've succeeded. Good on you. Another ten steps backward for womankind."

His hooded gaze narrowed. "I put women in the boardroom when they deserve it, Bailey. But I won't do it for appearance's sake. I think you're immensely talented and if you'd get over this ever-present need to prove yourself, you'd go far."

She refused to let the compliment derail her when he was never going to change. Pushing her hair out of her face, she glared at him. "I've outperformed every male in this company over the past couple of years, and that hasn't been enough. I'm through trying to impress you, Jared. Apparently the only thing that would is if I was a D cup."

His mouth tipped up on one side in that crooked smile women loved. "I don't think there's a man in Silicon Valley who would find you lacking in any department, Bailey. You just don't take any of them up on it."

The backhanded compliment made her draw in a breath. Sent a rush of color to her cheeks, heating her all over. She'd asked for it. She really had. And now she had to go.

"Here," she said, shoving the letter at him. "Consider this my response to your manifesto. And believe me, this was *draft two*."

He curled his long, elegant fingers around the paper and scanned it. Then deliberately, slowly, his eyes on hers, tore it in half. "I won't accept it."

"Be glad I'm not filing a human rights suit against you," she bit out and turned on her heel. "HR has the other copy. I'm giving you two weeks."

"I'm offering you the VP marketing job, Bailey." His words stopped her in her tracks. "You've done a phenomenal job boosting domestic sales. You deserve the chance to spread your wings."

Elation flashed through her, success after three long years of brutally hard work overwhelming her, followed almost immediately by the grounding notion of exactly what was happening here. She turned around slowly, pinning him to the spot with her gaze. "Which member of your team advised you to leverage me?"

If she'd blinked she would have missed the muscle that jumped in his jaw, but she didn't, and it made the anger already coursing through her practically flammable. "You want me," she stated slowly, "to be your poster child. Your token female executive you can throw in the spotlight to silence the furor."

His jaw hardened, silencing the recalcitrant muscle. "I want you to become my vice president of marketing, Bailey. Full stop. You've earned the opportunity, now take it. Don't be stupid. We're due at Davide Gagnon's house in the south of France the day after tomorrow to present our marketing plan, and I need you by my side."

She wanted to say no. She desperately wanted to throw the offer back in his face and walk out of here, dignity intact. But two things stopped her. Jared Stone was offering her the one thing she'd sworn she'd never stop working for until she got it—the chance to sit on the executive committee of a Fortune 500 company. And despite everything that he was—an impossible, arrogant full-of-himself jerk—he was the most brilliant brain on the face of the planet. And everyone knew it. If she worked alongside him as his equal she could write her ticket. Ensure she never went back to the life she'd vowed to leave behind forever.

Survival was stronger than her pride. It always had been. And men having all the power in her world wasn't anything unusual. She knew how to play them. How to beat them. And she could beat Jared Stone, too. She knew it.

She stared at him. At the haughty tilt of his chin. It was almost irresistible to show him how wrong he was. About her. About all women. This would be her gift to the female race...

"All right. On two conditions."

His gaze narrowed.

"Double my salary and give me the title of CMO."

"We don't have a chief marketing officer."

"Now we do."

His eyes widened. Narrowed again. "Bailey…"

"We're done then." She turned away, every bit prepared to walk.

"Fine." His curt agreement made her eyes widen, brought her swinging back around. "You can have both."

She knew then that Jared Stone was in a great deal of trouble. And she was in the driver's seat. But her euphoria didn't last long as she nodded and made her way past Mary's desk. There was no doubt she'd just made a deal with the devil. And when you did that, you paid for it.

CHAPTER TWO

By THE TIME newly minted CMO Bailey threw herself into a cab twenty-four hours later, bound for San Jose Airport and a flight to France, the furor over Jared Stone's manifesto had reached a fever pitch. Two feminist organizations had urged a full boycott of Stone Industries products in the wake of what they called his "irresponsible" and "repugnant" perspective on women. The female CEO of the largest clothing retailer in the country had commented on a national business news show, "It's too bad Stone didn't put this much thought into how he could balance out his board of directors, given that the valley is rife with female talent."

In response, a leading men's blog had declared Stone's manifesto "genius," calling the billionaire "a breath of fresh air for his honest assessment of this conflicted demographic."

It was madness. Even now, the cabbie's radio was blaring some inane talk show inviting men and women to call in with their opinions. She listened to one caller, a middle-aged male, praise Jared for his "balls" to take the bull by the horns and tell it like it was. Followed by a woman who called the previous caller "a caveman relic of bygone days."

"Please," Bailey begged, covering her eyes with the back of her hand, "turn it off. Turn the channel. Anything but him. I can't take it anymore."

The cabbie gave her an irritated glance through his grubby rearview mirror, as if he were fully on board with Jared's perspective and *she* was the deluded one. But he switched the channel. Bailey fished her mobile out of her purse and dialed the only person she regularly informed of her whereabouts in case she was nabbed running through the park some night and became a statistic.

"Where are you?" her best friend and former Stanford roommate, Aria Kates, demanded. "I've been trying to get you ever since this Jared Stone thing broke."

"On my way to the airport." Bailey checked her lipstick with the mirror in her compact. "I'm going with him to France."

"*France?* You didn't *quit*? Bailey, that memo is outrageous."

And *designed* for shock value. She shoved the mirror back in her purse, sat back against the worn, I've-seen-better-days seat, and pursed her lips. "He made me CMO."

"I don't care if he made you head of the Church of England.... He's an ass!"

Bailey stared at the lineup of traffic in front of them. "I want this job, Aria. I know why he promoted me. I get that he wants me to be his female executive poster child. I, however, am going to take this and use it for what it's worth. Get what I need, and get out."

Just as she'd done her entire life: clawed on to whatever she could grasp and used her talent and raw determination to succeed. Even when people told her she'd never do it.

She heard Aria take a sip of what was undoubtedly a large, extra-hot latte with four sweeteners, then pause for effect. "They say he's going to either conquer the world or take everyone down in a cloud of dust. You prepared for the ride?"

Bailey smiled her first real smile of the day. "Did I ever tell you why I came to work for him?"

"Because you're infatuated with his brain, Bails. And, I suspect, not only his brain."

Bailey frowned at the phone. "Exactly what does that mean?"

"I mean the night he hired you. He didn't start talking to you because he detected brilliance in that smart head of yours. He saw your legs across the room, made a bee-line for you, *then* you impressed him. You could almost see him turn off that part of his brain." Her friend sighed. "He may drive you crazy, but I've seen the two of you to-gether. It's like watching someone stick the positive and negative ends of a battery together."

She wrinkled her nose. "I can handle Jared Stone."

"That statement makes me think you're delusional.... Where in France, by the way?"

"Saint-Jean-Cap-Ferrat in the south."

"Jealous. Okay, well, have fun and keep yourself out of trouble. If you can with him along…"

Doubtful, Bailey conceded, focusing on the twelve-hour flight ahead with the big bad wolf. Admittedly, she'd had a slight infatuation with Jared when she joined Stone Indus-tries. But then he'd started acting like the arrogant jerk he was and begun holding her back at every turn, and after that it hadn't taken much effort at all to put her attraction aside. Because she was only at Stone Industries for one thing: to plunder Jared Stone's genius and move on.

The master plan hadn't changed.

Traffic went relatively smoothly for a Friday afternoon. Bailey stepped out of the cab in front of the tiny terminal for private flights, ready to soak up the quiet luxury from here on in. Instead she was blindsided by a sea of light, crisscrossing her vision like dancing explosions of fire. *Camera flashes*, her brain registered. She was stumbling to find her balance, her pupils dilating against the white lights, when a strong hand gripped her arm. She looked up to see Jared's impossibly handsome face set in grim lines.

"Good God," she muttered, hanging on to him as his security detail forged a path through the scrum. "Do you regret your little joke now?"

"I regretted it the minute it was broadcast to the world," he muttered, shielding her from a particularly zealous photographer. "But basking in regret isn't my style."

No, it wasn't…although looking amazing in the face of adversity was. Because in the middle of the jostling reporters, acting like a human shield for her, he looked all-powerful and infinitely gorgeous. His fitted dark jeans molded lean, powerful legs, topped by a cobalt-blue sweater that made his piercing blue eyes glitter in the late afternoon sun. And then there was his slicked-back dark hair he looked like he'd raked his hands through a million times that gave him a rebellious look.

When you tossed in the pirate-like scar twisting his upper lip, you ended up with a photo that would undoubtedly make front page news.

A photographer eluded Jared's two bodyguards, stepped in front of them and stuck a microphone in Bailey's face. "Kay Harris called you a figurehead this morning on her talk show. Any comment?"

One hundred percent true. Bailey gave the reporter an annoyed look as Jared started to push her forward. She leaned back against his arm, stood her ground and ignored his warning look. "I think," she stated, speaking to the cameras that had swung to her, "Mr. Stone made an error in judgment he apologized for earlier today and that's the end of the matter." She waved her hand at the man at her side. "I work for a brilliant company that is on a trajectory to become the world's top consumer electronics manufacturer. I couldn't be prouder of what we've accomplished. And I," she forced out, almost choking on the words, "have the utmost professional respect for Jared Stone. We have a great working relationship."

The questions came at her fast and furious. She held up a hand, stated they had a flight to catch, and let Jared propel her forward, hand at her back.

"Since when did you become such a diplomat?" he muttered, ushering her through the glass doors into the terminal.

"Since you created that *zoo* out there." She came to a halt inside the doors, took a deep breath and ran a hand over herself, straightening her clothing.

Jared did the same. Before the airline staff could spirit them off, he squared to face her. "Thank you. I owe you one."

Her gaze flickered away from the intensity of his. Looking at Jared was like observing all the major forces of the world stuffed inside the human form—charging him with an energy, a polar pull that was impossible to ignore. She'd felt it that night he'd headed purposefully across that bar and ended up hiring her. But she didn't need it now. Not when she'd gotten used to avoiding it. Not when she had to spend twelve hours crammed into a private jet with him absorbing it all.

"It was nothing," she muttered. "Don't make me regret saying it."

"I'm sure you already do…." His taunting rejoinder brought her head up. The dark glint in his eyes reminded her that there was still a line in this détente of theirs. And she knew there was. She really did. She just couldn't help it with him.

"After you," he murmured, extending his arm toward the exit to the tarmac. She swished past him out the doors and up the stairs of the sleek ten-person Stone Industries jet. She'd been on it once before, the decor a study in dark male sophistication. An official boarded the plane for a cursory check of their passports, and Bailey settled into one of the sumptuously soft leather seats and buckled up.

They took off, the powerful little jet racing down the runway, leaving San Jose behind in a blur of bright lights. As soon as the seat belt lights were turned off, Jared unpacked a mountain of paperwork and suggested they rehearse the presentation. He wanted it perfect—was determined to rehearse until they'd nailed every last key message. Given that it was new material to her, it might be a long night.

It was. Their styles were completely opposite. She liked to wing it. Jared, emphatically not. Not to mention how intimidating he was when his passion for the subject took over. She could usually hold her own with the best of them, but he was too smart, too intense and too sure of himself to make it easy. So she resorted to her default mechanism of asking a million questions. Knowing the material inside out. What was the logic behind that statistic? Why were they making that particular point here? And wasn't this information coming too soon? Shouldn't they save it to drive the stake in at the end?

Four hours and four rounds of the presentation later, Jared flung himself into the chair opposite her and rubbed his hands over his eyes. "This isn't working. You are the queen of going off script."

"It makes it believable," she countered, sinking down into her chair. "I'm playing off you, taking your lead. You're the one who keeps losing the thread."

He gave her a disbelieving look. "*I'm* following the slides."

She blew out a breath as her head pounded like a jackhammer. "You are stuck on *process*. Try loosening up. It works beautifully. It's even better when I have an audience."

He dropped his head into his hands. "That idea scares me. Greatly."

She looked longingly up at the flight attendant as she came to hover by them with an offer of predinner drinks. "I'm having a glass of wine. I've earned it."

"Whiskey," Jared muttered to the attendant, then sat back and watched her from beneath lowered lashes. The *longest* lowered lashes she'd ever encountered. Divine, really.

He opened them. "What is it about falling in line you have a problem with?"

Bailey widened her eyes. "I fall in line when I need to. Witness the press a few hours ago, for instance."

"You are challenging everything I say," he growled.

"I'm challenging everything that doesn't make sense," she countered. "I haven't seen the material before. I'm an objective eye."

"It's *perfect*."

"It *would be* perfect if everyone in the world thought exactly like you. Davide Gagnon has a creative streak. You need to appeal to that side of him."

"An expert on him already?" he asked darkly.

"I did my homework." She tore open the can of cashews she'd brought with her and shoved some in her mouth. "What value would I be adding if I fell into line like a trained seal?"

His expression inched darker. "A lot of value right now, given that this is the only rehearsal time we're going to get. Davide is famous for his social lifestyle. You can bet he'll have things lined up every night."

She winced inwardly. Although her research had told her all about Davide Gagnon's lavish lifestyle and love of a good party that tended to include the who's who of Europe, and she'd packed accordingly, it was the type of lifestyle she abhorred. She'd seen too much of it when she'd danced in Vegas. The destructive things money and power could do. And although she'd been the girl who'd always gone home after the show rather than take advantage of the high rollers who'd wanted to lavish hefty doses of it on her, she'd seen—*experienced*—enough of it for a lifetime.

Focus on her studies, fast-track her business degree and get the hell out. That had been her mantra.

"Bailey?"

Jared was looking at her, an impatient look on his face. She blinked. "Sorry?"

"I was saying Davide has a fondness for blondes." He folded one long leg over the other and popped a handful of the cashews into his mouth. "I consider you my secret weapon."

Hostility flared through her, swift and sharp, spurred by a past she couldn't quite banish. "If you're suggesting I flirt with him, that's not going to happen. And I can't believe you would even say that considering that your reputation is hanging by a thread and I'm the only thing keeping it afloat."

He gave her a long look as the attendant set their drinks on the table. "I was asking you to charm him, Bailey, not sleep with him."

She gave him a black look. "Forgive me for misinterpreting. We women apparently don't have a use beyond securing ourselves a rich man and keeping ourselves within the style *to which we've become accustomed*. So I just wanted to make the point."

A muscle jumped in his jaw. "You were the one who just said I'd made my apology and bygones should be bygones. Perhaps you can walk the walk, no?"

"That was for public consumption." She pulled the glass of deep ruby-red wine toward her. "Know that in my head, my respect for you personally is at an all-time low."

His eyes darkened to a wintry, stormy blue. "As long as your professional respect is intact, I'm not worried about your personal opinion."

And there it was. The man who cared about nothing but his driving need for success. He was legendary for it and she couldn't fault it because she was his mirror image.

She took a sip of the rich, velvety red, her palate marking it a Cabernet/Merlot blend. "I am curious about one thing, though."

He lifted a brow.

"What *is* your real opinion of women?"

His sexy, quirky mouth turned up on one side. "If you think I'm answering that, you consider me a stupider man than I am."

'No, really," she insisted, waving her glass at him. "Utterly open conversation. I want to know."

His long-lashed gaze held hers for a moment, then he shrugged. "I think the science of relationships goes back as far as time. As far as the cavemen… We men—we hunt, we gather. We provide. Women want us for what we can offer them. And as soon as we can't, as soon as they get a better offer," he drawled, "we are expendable."

She was shocked into silence. Considering that her mother had been the only thing keeping her family afloat with her alcoholic father off work more than on, that seemed ludicrous. "You can't really mean that," she said after a moment. "It's crazy to lump all women together like that."

He lifted a shoulder. "I never say anything I don't mean. You wonder who's really in the power position, Bailey? Think about it."

She frowned. "What about women who can provide for themselves? Women who bring equal billing to a relationship?"

"It doesn't survive. There is *always* a balance of power in a relationship. And when a woman has that power, the relationship is never going to last. Women *need* us to dominate. To be the provider."

She stared at him. "That's ridiculous. You are impossible."

His white smile glittered in the muted confines of the jet. "I've been called worse this week. Come on, admit it, Bailey. A strong woman like you must like a man to take control. Otherwise you'd walk all over him."

A warning buzzed its way along her temple, signaling dangerous territory she wasn't about to traverse. She lifted her chin, met his magnetic blue gaze head-on. "On the contrary. I like to be in control, just like you do, Jared. *Always*. Haven't you figured that out already?"

His lashes lowered, studying, *analyzing*. "I'm not sure I have one-fifth of you figured out."

The air between them suddenly felt too hot, too tight in the close confines of the jet that pulsed with the powerful throb of the engines. She took a jerky sip of her wine. "Should we get back to rehearsing?"

"After dinner." He nodded toward her glass. "Enjoy your wine. Be social."

She searched for something in the safe zone to talk about and when that didn't materialize, pulled her purse toward her, searched for her lipstick and fished it out to reapply.

"Don't."

Her hand froze midway to her face. "Sorry?"

"Don't reapply that war paint. You look perfect the way you are."

Heat spread through her, confusing in its intensity. He'd probably used that line on a million women. Why it made her drop the lipstick back into her purse and reach for her lip balm instead was unclear to her.

Jared sat back in his chair, tumbler balanced on his knee, hand sliding over his dark-shadowed jaw. "There's never a hair out of place, Bailey. Never a cuff that isn't perfectly turned or posture that isn't ramrod straight even after four hours of rehearsing." He angled an inquisitive brow at her. "Why the facade? What are you afraid people might find out if you relax?"

She angled her chin at him. "I work in the male-dominated, testosterone-driven world of Silicon Valley. Men will walk all over me if I show weakness. You of all people should know that."

"Perhaps," he agreed. "Is that why you turn them all down? Let them crash and burn for all to see?"

She looked him straight in the eye. "That would be their stupidity if I wasn't showing interest. And *this* would be my personal life. Which doesn't have any part in this conversation."

"Oh, but it does," he said softly, his gaze holding hers. "We need to go into this presentation like a well-oiled machine. Know each other inside out, anticipate each other's needs, move together seamlessly until we are a well-orchestrated symphony. Trust each other implicitly so no matter what they throw at us we've got it. But right now, we're a disjointed mess. The trust is lacking, and I don't feel like I know the first thing about you."

A chill stole through her. No one *knew* her. Except perhaps Aria. They knew Bailey St. John, the composed, successful woman she'd created by sheer force of will. A female version of the Terminator…and not even bulldog Jared was going to uncover the real her.

Which necessitated an act. And a good one. She cradled her wineglass against her chest, leaned back in her seat and slid into the interview persona she'd perfected over the years. "Ask away, then. What do you want to know?"

Jared leaned back in his seat and took in Bailey's deceptively relaxed pose. He had no doubt from her evasive answers that she was going to give him only half the story. But something was more than nothing, and their disastrous rehearsals necessitated some kind of synergy. They weren't connecting on any level except to strike sparks off each other. Which might be fine, desirable even, in the bedroom, but it wasn't helping here with the board breathing down his neck, the press all over him like a second skin and the most important presentation of his life looming.

If he and Bailey walked into that room right now and did the presentation, they would go down like the Titanic. Slowly and painfully. Davide Gagnon might have hand-picked them as partner, but it didn't mean they could afford to miss one detail about why he should work with them.

He took a long sip of his whiskey, considered her while it burned a comforting trail down his throat, then rested the glass on his thigh. "I was reviewing your résumé. Why the University of Nevada-Las Vegas for your undergrad? It seems an odd choice given your East Coast upbringing. Florida, right?"

She nodded.

"Did you win a scholarship?"

The closed-off look he'd watched her perfect over the years made a spectacular reappearance. "I'm from a small city outside Tampa called Lakeland. Population less than a hundred thousand. I wanted to go away to school, and UNLV had a good business program."

"So you chose Sin City?"

"Seemed as good a place as any."

"Did it have something to do with the fact that you aren't close to your family?"

"Why would you say that?"

"You never go home for the holidays and you never talk about them. So I'm assuming that's the case."

Her cool-as-ice blue eyes glittered. "I'm not particularly close to them, no."

Definitely a sore point. "After UNLV," he continued, "you did your MBA at Stanford, my alma mater, then went straight to a start-up. Did you always want to work in the Valley?"

She nodded. "I loved technology. I would have been an engineer if I hadn't gone into business."

"They're in high demand," he acknowledged. "Where did the interest come from? A parent? School?"

She smiled. "School. Science was my favorite class. My teachers encouraged me in that direction."

"And your parents," he probed. "What do they do?"

If he hadn't been watching her, studying her like a hawk, he would have missed the slight flinch that pulled her shoulders back. She lifted her chin. "My father is a traveling salesman and my mother is a hairdresser."

His eyes widened. Her less-than-illustrious background didn't faze him. The complete incompatibility with the woman in front of him did. He would have pegged her as an aristocrat. As coming from money. Because everything about Bailey was perfect. Classy. From the top of her glamorous platinum-haired head, to her finely boned striking features, to her long, lean thoroughbred limbs, she was all sophistication and impeccable taste.

"So no man, no family," he recounted. "Who do you spend your time with when you're not at work? Which is always…" he qualified.

"You should be happy I do that. It's why your sales numbers are so impressive."

"I like my employees to have a life," he countered drily. "Maybe you have a man tucked away none of us know about?"

"I have friends," she said stiffly.

"Pastimes? Hobbies?"

Silence. He watched her mind work, coming up with a suitable answer, not the real one. "I like to read."

"Ah yes," he nodded. "So home on a Friday night with a book in your hand? That sounds awfully dull."

"Maybe I import my men," she offered caustically. "Ship them in for a hot night, then send them home."

His mouth twisted. "Lucky guys."

"Jared…" She exhaled heavily. "Are you ever politically correct?"

"Hopefully this weekend, yes."

She smiled at that. "Is that enough information so we can move on to *your* fascinating backstory?"

"It'll do for now." He poured her another glass of wine, intent on loosening her up.

She shifted, tucked her legs underneath her. He kept his eyes off her outstanding calves with difficulty. "Is it true," she asked, running a finger around the rim of her glass, "that you got your love of electronics tinkering in the garage with your father?"

He nodded. "My father was an investment banker, but his true love was playing with a car's engine until the sun came down. I would go out to the garage and work alongside him until my mother made me come in."

She frowned. "You said *was*. Did your father pass?"

"No." He felt his defenses sliding into place like a cell door at Alcatraz, but opening up was a two-way street, and he needed to give, too. "He embezzled money from the bank, from his personal circle of friends, got himself in way too deep and tried to win it all back in a high-stakes game in Vegas."

Her eyes widened. "And they chewed him up?"

"Yes."

"I'm so sorry. I didn't know."

His mouth twisted. "It's not exactly in my bio. The bank did a good job of hushing it up, and only those close to it ever knew."

Her gaze moved uncertainly over his. Wondering why he'd told her.

"Trust," he said softly. "You shared with me. I need to

share with you. I meant what I said, Bailey. This is the most important presentation of Stone Industries' history. There are no second chances. We have to nail it. We have to trust each other completely walking into that room or we don't do it at all."

She chewed ferociously on her lower lip. He kept his gaze on hers. "You have to be all-in, Bailey."

She nodded. "I'm in."

His shoulders settled back into place, his relief palpable. "Good. Let's try to streamline that second section so it sings…"

She leaned forward to grab her notebook. "Ouch."

"What?"

She pressed her fingers to her neck. "I slept the wrong way last night. I've got the worst kind of kink."

She'd been struggling with it throughout their rehearsals, he realized. He'd thought her funny faces had been grimaces about the material but instead, she'd been in pain.

"Come here."

She looked blankly at him.

He held up his hands. "These are magic. Let me work it out so you can concentrate."

She shook her head. "It'll work itself out. Let's just figure that p—"

He got to his feet and pointed at the chair. "We need to nail this and you obviously can't concentrate. Five minutes."

She came then, taking the chair he'd vacated, as if she knew further resistance was futile. "Here," she told him, pointing to the spot. He sat down on the side of the chair, ran his fingers over her skin lightly, then with increasing pressure.

"Here?"

"Yes," she groaned. "Be careful. It's killing me."

"Trust, remember?" He set about working the immobilized muscles, on the outer edges first, loosening them up so he could find his way to the source of the pain. He felt her relax, let him in. But only so much. And he wondered how often, if ever, this woman allowed herself to be vulnerable?

I like to be in control, just like you do, Jared. Always.

Kink worked fully, he brought his hands down to her shoulders and started to work out the knots from where she'd held herself stiff from the pain. He expected her to protest. Say that was fine. But she didn't. And why the hell did he still have his hands on her?

The scent of her perfume filled his nostrils, light but heady. *Like her…* It made a fist coil tight in his chest. The air thickened around them, his hands slowing as he finished the job. She must have felt it too, this undeniable connection between them, because her breathing changed, quickened, a flush stained her alabaster skin, and she was completely pliable beneath his hands.

She wanted him.

Bailey St. John—queen of the brush-off—wanted him.

The vaguely shattering discovery took him to a place it wasn't wise to go. The woman every man in Silicon Valley coveted was not impenetrable. *No pun intended.* She was far from asexual as some had suggested jokingly, and perhaps bitterly. And it struck him that maybe he'd been avoiding working with her, promoting her, because he'd been afraid of *this*. Because they'd have to work hand in hand. Because he'd wanted to unravel the mystery that was Bailey St. John from the first day she'd walked into his office.

Correction. From the night he'd hired her…

His body tightened with an almighty surge of testosterone. Not particularly admirable, but there it was. And how had he not realized it sooner? Hadn't he learned this in grade school? You only fought with the girls you liked. And on a much more adult level, he realized he wanted

Bailey in his bed. *Under him* as he peeled back layer upon layer.

He would not be the one to crash and burn…

"Bailey?"

"Mm?" Her husky, pleasure-soaked tone rocked him to the core.

"I think I've figured out our issue."

"Our issue?"

"Mmm." He slid his fingers to the racing pulse at the base of her neck. "This."

CHAPTER THREE

BAILEY YANKED HERSELF out from under Jared's hands so fast she pretty much redid all the damage he'd just undone. Her hazy brain wasn't firing on all cylinders as she met her boss's glittering blue gaze, focused and intent, containing the same heated sexual awareness that had been fueling her unspeakable fantasy.

Hot and uncensored, it had been outrageously good...

"We— I—" She started to talk. Anything to deny what was happening.

Jared held up a hand. "There's only one thing that's called, Bailey: pure, unadulterated sexual attraction."

Her pulse racing, hectic color firing her cheeks, it was really pointless to deny it. But it would be insanity not to. "There goes your out-of-control ego again, Jared," she taunted, raising her chin. "You *antagonize* me, you drive me crazy, but you do not attract me."

His jaw hardened. The glitter in his eyes morphed into a spark of pure challenge as his *I am man*, chest-beating need to prove his masculinity roared to life. Her breath stopped in her lungs, her irrational desire to see what would happen if he did lose it mixing with her common sense to create a complete state of inertia. Then his dark lashes came down to shield his eyes, that superior control he exerted over himself sliding back into place. "I think," he said softly, "this is a case of semantics. Antagonize... Attract... What-

ever you want to call it—it's an issue. And we need to figure it out if we're going to make this presentation work. If
we're going to make this *partnership* work."

She pulled in a silent breath, using the reprieve to
steady herself. To regain her equilibrium. He was right.
She needed to figure this antagonism/attraction thing out
before she made a complete fool of herself. Before she destroyed this opportunity she'd been handed.

"How about," she offered, with as cool a gaze as she
could muster, "you try to be a little looser, go with the flow,
and I'll pay more attention to the script? I'm sure even *we*
can meet somewhere in the middle."

His mouth tilted up on one side. "It's worth a shot."

They dined on a delicious meal of filet mignon and
salad, Bailey severely curtailing her consumption of the
delicious wine so her head was clear. She'd made a serious
mistake in ever thinking she could let her defenses down
in front of Jared. In tipping her hand and revealing an attraction she hadn't even fully admitted to herself. But she'd
learned her lesson. And she wasn't about to do it again.

Their final rehearsal wasn't perfect, but it was a heck of
a lot better than their earlier attempts. She toned it down,
made a concerted effort to follow Jared's lead, and they
made it through in a fairly civilized way. Jared, being the
generous soul that he was, gave her a couple of hours'
sleep before they landed in the sparkling, glittering South
of France.

Just how luxurious their trip was going to be was apparent when upon their arrival in the Nice airport, they were
not met by a car, but a shiny silver helicopter flown by
Davide Gagnon's personal pilot. He jumped down under
the slowing, still-whirling helicopter blades, greeted them,
stowed their luggage in the back of the aircraft, and took
them on their way.

Their trip across the sun-kissed Côte d'Azur to the legendary Peninsula of Billionaires, in between Nice and Monaco, featured some of the most exclusive properties on the French Riviera. Bailey, who'd done the South of France on a budget in her backpacking days with Aria, was googly-eyed. Luxurious villas sat in secluded coves behind high cliffs that sheltered them from the wind. And the colors were glorious, brilliant fuchsia and purple-soaked gardens bordering the sparkling turquoise sea.

Jared gave her an amused look as she chatted with the pilot, extending her twenty-question strategy to him. It was presently a balmy twenty-one degrees Celsius, the pilot told them as he set the chopper down on the Gagnon property's private landing pad, expected to get much hotter over the weekend, just in time for film festival season in the South of France.

They were met outside the low, cream-colored sprawling villa that sat directly on the bay by Davide Gagnon's head housekeeper, who informed them their host was en route home from a business meeting and would greet them that night at the party. Until then, they were free to explore the grounds and beach and enjoy some lunch. Bailey forced some salad into her jet-lagged body, took one look at her oceanfront suite—situated directly beside Jared's at one end of a wing—and elected for a face-plant into the three-hundred-count Egyptian cotton sheets and an afternoon nap.

When she woke, the brilliant afternoon sun had faded into early evening, and a sensual pink-orange sunset was streaking its way across the sky. She yawned, padded to her terrace and watched as it deepened into a hot-pink fire laced with smoky gray-blue. She would have done just about anything to be able to sit there and enjoy the magnificent view with a glass of the wine on ice in her suite, but it was already close to six. She needed to shower, dress and face the jeweled, exquisitely coutured guests of Davide Gagnon in a half hour. And hope she had learned enough over the years to fake it so her lowbrow, uncouth roots didn't show through like an ugly weed in a sea of mimosa and lavender.

Put her in a boardroom matched against the world's nastiest deal-maker, and she was rock solid. Put her in a social situation like tonight, and she needed all her acting skills to survive. Etiquette training had only taught her which fork to use. Which wine to drink with what. It didn't make her one of them. And it never would.

She gazed out at the explosion of color in the sky and reminded herself parties like this were about working a room. If there was anything she'd learned as a dancer, it was that. How to get what she wanted out of the men who'd come to watch her so she could make a different life for herself. And tonight was no different. She needed to focus on the prize, Davide Gagnon. Use what she'd learned about him, what she knew of men like him, to convince him a Stone Industries partnership was his ticket to European sales domination.

Show Jared he'd been overlooking a valuable asset for a very long time.

Once she got over her nerves...

She reluctantly abandoned the gorgeous view and stepped inside. She might not be able to enjoy the sunset, but she *could* indulge in a glass of wine to ease the tension. Pouring herself a glass, she took it into the stunning marble bathroom, stepped under a hot shower, and systematically washed away the old Bailey and installed the new one in her place.

Wrapping herself in the thick, soft robe that hung on the door, she padded into the dressing area and ran her fingers over the whisper-soft silks and taffetas she'd hung in the wardrobe. But there was never any question as to which she'd pick. She pulled the just-above-the knee beaded champagne-colored cocktail dress from the hanger and slipped it on. The dress was the softest silk, hugging every curve with just the right amount of propriety. Sexy but conservative at the same time.

She surveyed herself in the floor-length mirror. There was nothing cheap about the woman who looked back at her. This was not the twenty-dollar designer knockoff dress that had once been the only thing she could afford. And it showed.

Working her hair into a smooth, shimmering mass of curls with a round brush and a dryer, she topped it with minimal eye makeup and gloss. Enough to highlight her features. She had just added a dash of perfume to her pulse points when a knock sounded at the connecting door. *Jared.*

She moved across the room, undid the bolt and opened the door. The sight of her boss in an exquisitely tailored black tux might have been more intimidating than the prospect of the evening ahead. From the tip of his slicked-back dark hair to his freshly shaven jaw and long-limbed masculinity, he was devastating.

Jared followed Bailey into her suite, her barefoot, wine-in-her-hand invitation to come in doing something strange to his insides. Her dress—what would you call it, champagne-colored?—hugged every curve as if it had been sewn onto her. Curves that could burn themselves into your memory if you let them. Her hair fell in smooth gold waves to her shoulders, one side pushed back with a diamond butter-fly clasp. Her exquisite face held only the faintest trace of war paint. But she was the most beautiful woman he'd ever stepped foot into a room with. That he knew.

He attempted to divert his wayward thoughts with a thoughtful look down at the floor tapestry, and instead treated himself to a perfect view of her long golden legs, ruby-tipped toes sinking into the carpet. And felt himself lose the plot completely. If she'd been a woman he was dating, he would have skipped the cocktails entirely. Insisted she share her wine while they watched the sunset together, taken the dress off her with his teeth and made her come at least twice before they joined the others.

And that didn't take into account what he would have done to her after the night was over.

He would have had her until sunrise.

"Jared?"

He coughed and lifted his gaze to hers. "Sorry?"

A pink stain stole over her cheeks. "The gold or champagne shoes?"

He looked at the two pairs of sky-high heels dangling by her fingertips and decided either of them would make every man in the room tonight want to bed her.

"Gold," he muttered. "It'll contrast with the dress."

"Right." She tossed the other pair on the carpet, braced her hand against the wall and slipped the stilettos on. As his hormone-clouded brain cleared, he noticed the tight set of her face. The way her ramrod straight posture seemed to have pulled up another centimeter. How she picked up the glass of wine and downed the remainder with a jerky movement reminiscent of his father on the nights he'd had to attend the bank functions he'd never been comfortable with, except his drink had been scotch.

The chink in her armor confounded him. "Are you nervous? You know the plan. We find out Maison's strategy when it comes to the environment and we're all set. It's the last missing piece."

A stillness slipped across her fine-boned face. Indecipherable. "I've got the plan down, Jared. I'm fine."

He didn't buy it for a second. Her revelations on the plane had illuminated one thing about Bailey. She hadn't been born into this lifestyle. She did a good job making it look as though she had, but she hadn't.

He stepped closer, something about her vulnerability touching him deep down inside. "Don't you know?" he said softly, looking down at her. "You're always the most beautiful woman in the room, Bailey. *And* the smartest."

A small smile twisted her lips before she wrinkled her nose at him. "I'll bet that line works wonders for you."

"You have no idea." His answering grin was self-effacing. "But I've never meant it more than I do now. So be yourself tonight, and you'll knock them dead."

She studied him for a moment. Nodded. "We should go."

For what reason he didn't know, he braved her prickly exterior and wrapped his fingers around her delicate hand instead of offering his arm.

"Ready?" he asked roughly.

"Ready."

They emerged on the buzzing wraparound terrace of the villa, ablaze with light and laughter on the warm Mediterranean night, where perhaps close to fifty people had already gathered, cocktails in hand. As Jared cased the crowd, he noticed an Academy Award-winning producer to his left, a high-profile A-list Hollywood couple to his right, and wasn't that Roberto Something-or-other, the Italian film director known for his sprawling epics, straight ahead? The big personalities had, apparently, all made it into town.

He grabbed a couple of glasses of champagne from a passing waiter's tray and handed one to Bailey. Gagnon had spared no expense: a quartet playing in a corner of the large, floodlit deck, black-jacketed staff circulating like an efficient swarm of bees, and from what he'd heard, a well-known French singer slated to play later in the evening, purportedly a mistress to one of the French cabinet ministers. But Jared had only one goal in mind. To corner Davide Gagnon and get the information he needed to develop that final, crucial piece of strategy.

He did not miss the attention every man at the party paid to the woman by his side as he picked out Gagnon, placed a palm to Bailey's back and led her through the crowd. There were a lot of beautiful, stunning even, women at the party. Bailey outshone them all, glittering like a glamorous Hollywood icon brought forward to the present, outclassing even the real Hollywood A-listers in attendance if you were to ask his opinion. But in true Bailey style, she ignored them all and focused on their target.

Davide Gagnon detached himself from the group he was standing with and came toward them, his sun-lined, handsome, younger-looking-than-he-was face breaking into a wide smile as he took Bailey's hand and brought it to his mouth. "My pilot told me you were lovely," he murmured gallantly. "I think he erred on the conservative side."

Bailey gave their host a warm smile and returned his greeting. *In French.* In perfectly accented, lilting Parisian French that sounded so sexy Jared's jaw dropped open.

"I think I'm in love," Davide murmured, hanging on to her hand. "What are you doing with the most controversial man in the room, *ma chère?*"

"And the most brilliant," Bailey returned smoothly as she drew back, an amused sparkle lighting her blue eyes. "I'm with him for his brain."

Jared's gaze tangled with hers. She appreciated a lot more than his brain, he was sure of it. And he suddenly had the burning urge to make her admit it. Maybe it was the look of pure male appreciation on Davide's face. Maybe it had been the scene with the shoes. Regardless, it was out of the question. He had to be a good boy. He was on a very short leash with no room for error.

"You have an absolutely magnificent home," he murmured appreciatively, when Davide finally deigned to let go of Bailey's hand and offer him his. "Thank you for the invitation to join you."

"It only increased the desirability of my guest list," the distinguished Frenchman said in a wry tone. "Like you or hate you, they all want to meet you."

Jared caught the disapproval the Frenchman lobbed him loud and clear. "It was a personal joke that should never have been made public," he asserted.

"But it was," Davide drawled. "And now you've alienated fifty percent of the population."

Tension tightened his jaw. "It will blow over."

Gagnon's eyes glinted. "That's what Richard Braydon thought when his comments about the French were broadcast on YouTube." His gaze was deliberate. "It destroyed his business."

A fist reached in and wrapped itself around his heart. Gagnon could not have missed the business stories depicting him teetering on a high-wire when it came to retaining control of his company. His radical push in a direction few dared to go. The Frenchman's deal would push him over the edge one way or another, and Davide knew it.

"It *will* blow over," Jared reiterated harshly. "And when you see what we have in our marketing plan, you will not have any doubts, I promise you."

The other man inclined his head. "I expect brilliance from you, Stone. It's the wild cards you throw my way I'm not so sure about."

Jared gritted his teeth as Gagnon blew off the conversation and turned to introduce them around. Turned to introduce *Bailey* around, if he were to be accurate. With himself in Davide's bad books, she apparently was a more enticing draw.

He spent the rest of the cocktail hour deflecting conversation of his manifesto, which truly seemed to have struck a global note. Heartily sick of it and inordinately annoyed with himself, he was then seated next to Gagnon's daughter, Micheline, for dinner. Whether a joke or penance on Davide's part, Jared thought he'd died and gone to hell by the main course. Micheline had not let up over the soup and appetizers about how damaging his effort "to be cute" was to women. How much it denigrated everything she'd worked for.

By the time the Cornish hens came, he would have laid down on the floor and allowed her to stick needles in every part of him if she would have stopped. *Just stopped.*

Bailey, of course, had been placed beside Davide. She spent the evening chatting away to him in that perfect French he didn't understand so he couldn't follow their conversation. Apparently, she had lost her nerves.

Micheline glanced over at her father and Bailey, her thin mouth curving in a cynical smile. "She was a brilliant stroke of strategy on your part, Jared, no doubt about it. You know Daddy can't resist a beautiful blonde."

"She's extremely smart," Jared muttered. And annoying. *He needed* to be in on that conversation. But it didn't happen. Dessert stretched into liqueurs and no one moved. Finally, the French singer took the stage on the terrace, the band backing her up, and Jared seized the opportunity to grab his CMO.

"Care for a dance?" he requested on a slightly belligerent note, holding out his hand.

She nodded and excused herself from Davide's side. Jared's long strides ate up the distance to the dance floor set up on a corner of the balcony. He slid an arm around Bailey's waist, laced his fingers through hers and pulled her to him.

"When were you planning on including me in your little party?"

She absorbed that, absorbed his frustration, then sighed. "You told me to work him, Jared. That's what I'm doing."

"*Awfully* well."

She sealed her bottom lip over her top.

"When were you going to tell me you spoke French?"

"That was also on my résumé," she said pointedly. "Along with the fact that I speak Spanish and Italian."

"I have a feeling that résumé of yours isn't worth the paper it's printed on," he said darkly, inhaling that trademark floral scent of hers. Trying to ignore what she'd look like stripped of that dress, what his psyche had been working on all evening. "What other tricks do you have up your sleeve? Just so I have a heads-up."

Her perfectly arched brows came together. "I know it must be disconcerting that Davide's being a bit cool with you, but you can't blame me for that."

"I'm not blaming you, I'm wondering *who you are*. You whip out this perfect French I didn't know you speak then you're off talking about Plato over dinner."

"I studied that in college. He's Davide's favorite philosopher."

"Of course he is. He's also clearly besotted with you."

Her calm look hardened until she was matching him stare for stare. "I am using my brain, Jared. Something the women you consort with likely don't do. I can understand why you would find that hard to appreciate."

"*I* appreciate your brain."

"Right." She echoed his skepticism. "He's revealing a lot. I'm getting some good insight into how his brain works. I've run some ideas by him and—"

"You've *run some ideas by him?*" Fury twisted his insides. "I don't want you running ideas by him, I want you *sticking to the script.*"

Her lips pressed together. "He liked them. Loved them, in fact."

He kept a leash on himself as the urge to explode like an overdue volcano rolled over him. "Which ideas are we talking about? The ones in our presentation or your rogue *thoughts?*"

Hot color dusted her cheeks. "One of mine—the one about the kiosks in the yoga studios…"

He uttered a curse. "That is not in our plan. It is nowhere in our plan, nor is it going to be. You need to put a leash on yourself."

She lifted her chin, her blue eyes a stormy gray. "He loved the idea, Jared. He said it was exactly where his head was at. So maybe *you* need to open your mind. Use your imagination."

"I am using my imagination," he came back shortly, his gaze sliding over the dress, the *curves* every man in the room hadn't been able to take his eyes off of all night. "And I don't like where it's taking me."

She swallowed, a visible big gulp. "Do not do that. We are negotiating a business deal here, remember? Focus."

"I am focusing," he countered silkily. "Like every other male at this party, you have my complete attention in that dress. Now what are you going to do with it?"

Her eyes widened. Fire arced between them, swift and strong. It made his blood tattoo through his veins in a triumphant march. Sent heat lancing through his body. Bailey stared back at him like a deer caught in the headlights for a long moment. Then she blinked and stepped out of his arms.

"Walk away," she said softly. "You know the magazines are right about you, Jared. You're the one who needs a leash. You *are* out of control. You *have* lost your focus. You might think about getting it back. Think about what's actually going to win this rather than your own ego."

He stood there, hands clenched by his sides with the need to strangle her. She started off, then turned back with a final, parting shot.

"Green is only a peripheral strategy for Davide. He recognizes the importance to consumers, but he also knows they aren't willing to pay a premium for it. It's the price of entry."

She left before he could say anything. Wound her way back through the crowd. And he wondered if she was right. Was he out of control? Had he lost the thread? Because all he'd ever wanted to do was build a company that created great products. That made the impossible possible. But now that he'd done that, now that he was close to the pinnacle of success, he was doing everything but. He was glad-handing politicians, massaging a board's ego, weighing in on a marketing strategy he shouldn't have to worry about. About as far from the business of inspiration as you could get.

It was making him crazy.

He acknowledged one more thing before he bit out a curse and followed Bailey through the crowd. The yoga kiosk idea was brilliant. He'd thought that when she'd mentioned it, but final rehearsals weren't any time to be going off script.

Hell. He'd told Sam this would happen. He should have listened to his instincts.

Bailey spent the rest of the evening trying to manage the thundercloud that was Jared. She had the distinct feeling Davide Gagnon was administering a slap on the hand to her boss by giving him the cold shoulder, because there was no doubt that he respected Jared immensely.

She felt as if she was doing damage control on all sides. She also felt that she was the missing piece of the puzzle. The link between Jared's brilliance and Davide's creative side. Davide *loved* her ideas. He thought they were grassroots, buzz-inducing genius. And it made her feel just this side of cocky as she stood at the two men's sides for a last brandy as the crowd dwindled on the star-strewn terrace.

She felt *empowered.*

"My son, Alexander, has been delayed until tomorrow night," Davide updated them, pointing his glass at Jared. "Since he will be assuming the mantle at Maison upon my retirement next year, I want him to take the lead on this partnership decision. Why don't you enjoy the day tomorrow, meet Alexander at dinner and we can hear the presentation on Sunday?"

Jared, who had been raring to get the presentation nailed and over with, nodded congenially as if that were the greatest idea in the world.

"You're planning on stepping back over the next few months and transitioning, then?"

Davide nodded. "But I will still be very involved. My son is nothing if not ambitious and aggressive, but he'll need guidance." He shot Jared an amused look. "You'll like him. He likes to win as much as you do."

Jared smiled. "Not a bad trait." But his eyes were blazing with a plan. Four or five more hours of endless rehearsal? She almost groaned out loud at the thought. She might kill him first.

"I should say goodbye to a guest," Davide observed, "then I think I'm going to turn in. I'll see you in the morning for breakfast."

Bailey couldn't imagine anything better than bed. It was 2:30 a.m., her feet were killing her from the heels, she was jet-lagged, and the mental exhaustion of maintaining such a perfect facade all night, of using the French she hadn't practiced in years, had fried her brain. And then there was Jared, who moved silently beside her into the house like a quiet, lethal animal ready to strike.

She stayed quiet because taunting the animal was never a good strategy. And she'd slipped during that dance. Had gotten caught up in him for a split second before she'd walked away.

She didn't think that was helping their harmony.

The hallway stretched long and silent ahead of them. Jared stopped in front of her door, turned the handle and pushed it open. She came to a halt beside him, tension raking over her as she risked a look up at him. Latent, unresolved antagonism stretched like a live wire between them, Jared's penetrating stare making her shift her weight to the other foot. *Away* from him.

She pulled in a breath. "I shouldn't have said wh—"

Her heart sped into overdrive as he leaned forward and braced a hand against the wall behind her, his intent, purposeful look stopping the breath in her chest.

"Add the yoga idea to the deck, Bailey. Blow it out big and make it sing. And don't ever, *ever* run a strategy by a client without my approval first. Or you'll have the shortest tenure an executive at Stone Industries has ever seen."

He had removed his hand from the wall, stepped back and slammed his way into his room before her breath started moving again. She stood there, frozen for about five good seconds, then closed the door behind her. She backed up against the wood frame and finally let a triumphant smile curve her lips.

She had won. She had forced Jared Stone to acknowledge her ideas had merit. Not only had merit—they were going to present them to Davide Gagnon.

The smile faded from her lips, adrenaline pounding through her, licking at her nerve endings. Just now, outside that door, for a split second, she'd been convinced Jared was going to kiss her. Worse, for a fraction of that second, she had been unbearably excited by the idea.

Pulling in a breath, she wiped the back of her hand against her mouth. Since when had she become a fan of Russian roulette? Because surely that's what tonight had been.

With her own career at stake.

She might want to start thinking up alternative strategies.

CHAPTER FOUR

BAILEY WOKE UP full of "piss and vinegar" as her mother would have said, ready to attack the presentation, slot in her yoga idea and rehearse it until it sparkled. She pulled on shorts and a knit top, her mouth curving at the thought of her colorful mother. She may have limited her exposure to the family who'd turned her out when she'd started dancing, *stripping* as her father had bitingly referred to it, but it didn't mean she didn't have *some* good memories of her childhood.

She'd often spent Saturdays sitting on one of the worn, ripped leather chairs in her mother's hair salon rather than face the uncertain mood of her father—who could be even-keeled if he hadn't drunk too much that day, or downright mean if he had. She'd finish her homework, then sit fascinated as her mother's less-than-polished clientele talked about men, other women in an often catty fashion and anything else on their mind they felt needed to be aired. Eye-opening and illuminating conversation for a ten-year-old, to be certain. She'd made sure she didn't miss one juicy detail.

Unfortunately the glow hadn't lasted. As she'd gotten older, it was her mother's quietness she'd noticed. How she would listen but not talk much. Smile but not really. And she'd wondered if her mother knew what *she* knew. That her husband was not only a violent drunk who couldn't get over the loss of his high school football glory, but he'd also been unfaithful to her while on the road selling vacuum cleaners across the state. Bailey had answered one too many phone calls at home while her mother was working from a supposed "customer" named Janine not to put two and two together when her father subsequently ordered her out of the room and a hushed conversation ensued.

As a teenager, the glow had disappeared completely. What did it matter if her mother treated her to hot rollers on Saturday, if on Monday the clothes you wore to school were falling apart? When no one wanted to hang out with you because you were the epitome of poor *uncool?*

The memories floated in the window of her beautiful Cap-Ferrat suite, in blinding contrast to her current circumstances. She pressed her lips together, secured her hair in an elegant pile on top of her head, a hairstyle her mother would have called "hoity-toity," then made her way downstairs to join Davide and Jared in the breakfast room. The two men were discussing a trip into Nice to visit an art gallery. Davide stood, brushed a kiss across both of her cheeks and held a chair out for her. "Would you like to come with us, *ma chère?* The Chagalls are phenomenal."

"It's tempting," she responded, taking a seat. "But no thank you, I have work to do."

Jared murmured a greeting. She slid him a wary glance as she reached for the coffeepot. He was freshly shaven and annoyingly edible in a pair of jeans and a T-shirt that hugged his muscular chest and shoulders in all the right places. And more relaxed this morning if the softer edges of his face were anything to go by. She poured herself a full cup of the strong French brew. He'd probably been up at five doing his Buddhist meditation thing. Rumor had it he'd spent three months as a college dropout in India studying with a Zen master, and practiced it regularly. She'd even heard some of the engineers moan that Jared was on another tangent with his simplicity-inspired principles and they might never leave the lab with an end product if he didn't back off.

She removed her gaze from all that drool-inducing masculinity and focused on buttering a croissant. Rule number one when it came to her new strategy of handling Jared. No drooling. At all. Ignore him completely.

He and Davide took off to Nice in one of the Frenchman's vintage sports cars. Seduced by the spray of the waves and the chance to be outdoors, Bailey settled herself on one of the terraces overlooking the ocean, slid on some sunscreen and set to work building her slides.

By early afternoon, she had fleshed out her ideas into a compelling global strategy to catch consumers where they spent their free time. The kiosks to sell Stone Industries' wearable technologies—pulse monitors, odometers, fitness watches—onsite at yoga studios was only the first niche she was proposing. She added in examples of other health and fitness environments it could replicated in, reviewed the slides, then called it done with a satisfied nod.

This was her chance to shine. She'd forced Jared's hand in allowing her to include her ideas, now she had to make them worthy.

Turning her face up to the sun, she allowed herself a bit of downtime until the men came back.

Jared returned from Nice in his best mood of the week. He had bonded with Davide over their mutual love of art and managed to convince him that no, he was not dangling over the side of a cliff at Stone Industries with the board ready to cut him loose. He had also gone a long way to convincing him that there was little danger of long-term fallout from his manifesto with female consumers. People had short memories. Stone Industries would come out with its next big product and women would flock to it for its cool factor as they always did. And all of this would be a blip on the radar of a soon-to-be successful partnership.

The only thing that *was* messing with his superior mood was the email he'd gotten from his head of IT earlier this morning about the leak of his manifesto. It had literally stopped him in his tracks to discover after a cyber-chase of epic proportions, the email hack had been traced to the servers of Craig International. Which could only mean that Michael Craig, one of his most vocal critics on the Stone Industries board, was behind it. Had meant to bury him at a time of weakness. And for that, he decided, mouth set, stomach hard, as he went outside in search of Bailey, he would pay richly. He had never liked or trusted Michael Craig, had never felt they were playing on the same team. He would use this opportunity to get rid of him.

A growl escaped his throat as he headed toward the ocean-side terrace. You didn't mess with a man's lifeblood. That was way, way over the line.

He found Bailey on the terrace in a sun chair, laptop on her thighs, eyes closed, face turned up to the sun. Davide had gone on about how much he liked her on the drive to Nice. Not surprising after last night, but what *had* caught him off guard was that the collector of women, who'd lost his wife to illness at forty-five, had been focused not on Bailey's looks, but on her intelligence. Her creativity. He loved her—that much was obvious.

His mouth twisted as he surveyed her deceptively re-laxed pose on the lounger, long legs kicked out in front of her. He had no doubt her mind was going a mile a minute under those closed lids. That she wasn't sleeping but strat-egizing. And a sour feeling tugged at his gut. He'd side-lined her. Put her aside as a problem he didn't have time to deal with when it was his attraction to her that had been the issue all along. It wasn't like him to put the personal before business, and he hated that he had.

She opened her eyes, the wariness he'd witnessed this morning making a reappearance. "Did you have a good trip?"

"I did." He sank into the chair opposite her and poured himself a glass of her mineral water. "I owe you an apology."

Her eyes rounded. "For what?"

"For underestimating you. For letting you languish in a role that was beneath you."

She pushed herself up in the chair, her gaze meeting his. "We haven't done the presentation yet."

"I've seen your ideas." He took a long swallow of the water and sat back, resting the glass on his thigh. "I was wrong about you. I should have given you a voice." He lifted his shoulders. "Maybe you were right last night. Maybe my judgment has been off. It's been a David-and-Goliath battle with the board."

She pushed her finger into her cheek, a slow smile curving her lips. "I think I'm just going to say thank you and leave it at that. Are you sure you're feeling all right?"

A wry smile edged his mouth. "As a matter of fact, I am. You got me thinking last night. In a good way."

A frown marred her brow. "I might have been a bit harsh."

He shrugged. "I needed to hear it. I haven't had any time to think lately, and that's when I get myself into trouble."

She pointed toward her computer screen. "Want to see my slides?"

He nodded. "I've heard Alexander is a stickler for detail. He likes to wade into the minutiae—a bit of a control freak. So I want to ensure all our ducks are in order."

They went through the slides. He loved the way she'd laid them out, made a few suggestions of his own, and in a feat that could be classified as the eighth wonder of the world, they did a perfect run-through.

Satisfied the presentation was as smooth and as flawless as it was going to get, he challenged Bailey to a tennis game. She wasn't half bad. What she lacked in skill, she made up for in determination. Which seemed to be her modus operandi. She'd used the incredibly sharp brain she'd been born with, worked brutally hard and taken herself places.

He studied her as he waited for her to serve, concentration written across her face. Pictured her slugging it out at the local café, serving coffee all evening to put herself through school. Selling fifty pairs of shoes a day at the local mall to secure her future. And he couldn't help but admire her.

There was a lot of substance to Bailey St. John.

Bailey was still on a high when she pulled on white capri jeans, a body-hugging tank and a gauzy sheer blouse over it for their dinner at sea. Alexander Gagnon, Maison Electronique's director of international development and soon-to-be CEO, had flown in by helicopter while she'd been showering, the whir of the blades deafening as he'd touched down with two of Maison's other senior marketing staff. Tonight they would get to know the three executives over dinner on Davide's yacht, in a trip up the coast to Cannes. And tomorrow they would present their ideas to the group.

Much more comfortable with the intimate choice of setting this evening, Bailey slipped on strappy, glittery sandals, spritzed on a headier perfume for nighttime and met Jared *outside* his door. A slow smile curved his mouth when he opened it, denting his cheeks with those to-die-for almost-dimples. "You aren't going to let me pick your shoes?"

She resolutely ignored the sexy indentations. "I had it under control tonight."

His gaze swept over her, smooth and all-encompassing. "You look like you're channeling Grace Kelly."

She shifted her weight to the other foot. "I'll take that as a compliment."

The hand he placed at her back to ostensibly guide her down the hallway burned into her skin. "Do that," he murmured, bending so his softly spoken words rasped across the sensitive skin behind her ear. He looked pretty gorgeous himself in casual black pants and a short-sleeved dark blue shirt that made the most of his eyes. But she'd keep that to herself.

A small powerboat was waiting at the dock to take them out to the yacht. All the others were already on board, the crew member told them, firing the motor. Bailey took it all in, eyes wide. Growing up on a swamp in Florida, she'd been around boats her whole life. She'd seen the cruise ships lined up in Tampa when they'd visited the city. But that was a world away from this. Davide's yacht was at least seventy feet in length, they were about to cruise to Cannes during film festival time, and it frankly seemed unreal.

As they neared the sleek yacht painted in the blue, white and red colors of the French flag, the powerboat slowed to a crawl. They pulled alongside the yacht and were helped aboard by crew members. The rosy sky descended low over them, the lights of Saint-Jean-Cap-Ferrat twinkling from the shore as she stood looking back from the deck. It was glorious.

Davide greeted them, then turned to introduce them to the three men beside him. She greeted the two marketing executives who had flown in from Paris, then Alexander Gagnon, a tall, distinguished male with dark hair and cold-as-flint gray eyes.

Her pulse flatlined as Alexander stepped forward. She teetered on her sandals and would have stumbled backward if Jared hadn't placed a hand to her back and steadied her. *It couldn't be. It could not be.*

Her gaze moved over him, hungry to prove herself wrong. But the cold, hard eyes that had studied her, eaten her up with an unflinching need to have her those nights in Vegas almost ten years ago, were unmistakable. And he didn't miss a beat.

"How lovely to meet you...*Bailey*," he murmured, taking her hand to brush a kiss across her knuckles. "Alexander Gagnon."

Her breath constricted in her chest, a solid lump that threatened to choke her. She had never told him her real name. Had never told any of the men she danced for her real name. And now he knew it. She registered the fact with the almost hysterical need to turn around, jump off the boat and swim for shore.

Whether her body actually turned in that direction or whether Jared felt the shudder that went through her at the touch of Alexander Gagnon's lips on her skin, she wasn't sure. He released her for a moment to shake the other man's hand, then returned his palm to her back and kept it there. Alexander's gaze tracked the movement, then moved back to her face.

"I'm looking forward to your presentation tomorrow," he drawled. "Davide has been telling me about your great ideas."

Bailey's knees were shaking so hard she had to lean into Jared to keep herself upright. She felt his gaze hard on her, but kept hers focused straight ahead. Alexander was staring at her, waiting for a response. "Yes, well, we—" she stumbled "—we're hoping you'll like them."

"We know you'll *love* them," Jared corrected firmly, his palm pressing into her spine.

Alexander's lips twisted in a smile that didn't quite reach his eyes. "I've spent some time in the States. Davide mentioned you did your MBA at Stanford," he said to Bailey. "Where did you do your undergrad?"

He knew exactly where she'd done her undergrad. A fine sheen of perspiration broke out on her brow. Her voice dry, more gravelly than she'd ever heard it, she forced out, "At UNLV."

He snapped his fingers. "That must be it. I feel we've met before, but I can't place it. I've entertained a lot of clients in Vegas."

Every muscle in her body froze. The dark glitter in his eyes chilled her to the bone. "You must be mistaken," she rasped, finding her voice. "I'm quite sure we've never met."

Gauntlet laid, she lifted her chin. Alexander inclined his head. "My mistake, then."

She let out the breath she'd been holding. Requested a martini for the pure, unadorned hit of alcohol it would provide. Jared leaned down to her. "What is *wrong* with you?"

"I'm just not feeling…quite right."

His penetrating blue gaze ate through her. "A martini might not be the best thing, then. Let me get you some water."

"I'm fine," she said sharply. "It's probably just the boat. I'll get over it."

The martini helped. She sipped it, feeling the alcohol inject itself into her bloodstream, bite into the unreality gripping her. She had to find a way through this that didn't involve jumping off the boat and getting as far away from that man as she could. She had to pull herself together. *But how?* He had definitely recognized her. Her mind riffled through the options, desperately, not entirely clearly. She had to continue to pretend she'd never met him. Treat him as if he was just a business acquaintance. But it was just her luck that Alexander was seated across from her at dinner. And the red shirt he had on made it impossible to forget the last time she'd seen him.

She'd danced in her signature red lace dress and underwear as Kate Delaney that night at the Red Room—the highest-end strip club in Vegas, legendary for its beautiful women and sumptuous interiors. To wear red and dance last meant she was the owner's favorite, the most requested dancer of the week. Which wasn't unusual for her. She pulled in a ton of regulars who came to see her cool, untouchable beauty uncovered; to watch the sensual, erotic transformation unfold.

None of them could have known it was all an act for their benefit. That it was as far from the real Bailey as you could get.

Alexander Gagnon had sat in the front row that night. As he had every night for the past three. She'd felt his eyes on her, dark and unmoving. Despite the fact that there had been at least a hundred and fifty other men in the club, she had only been conscious of him. Of the tall, dark figure who had approached her each night to have a drink with him and whom she'd turned down flat despite the money he'd thrown at her, because there was something about the exquisitely dressed stranger with his thousand-dollar ties that said red light to her.

That night she had retreated to the dressing room, strangely affected by the intensity of the experience. The magnitude of the tip Alexander had left her. Her fellow dancers had showered and dressed in a mad rush to hit the town. Since she'd just been heading home to study for an exam the next day, Bailey had taken her time, sat at her dressing table and removed her thick, dramatic makeup. At some point she'd looked up to find the tall dark stranger standing inside the doorway. That all the other girls had gone. If you were to look past the dangerous edge to him that smoldered just below the surface, she would have called him inordinately handsome. Distinguished. But all she could smell was the scent of her own fear as she got to her feet, heart pounding.

"You can't be in here."

He'd lifted a brow. "Bruno owes me one. He gave us five minutes."

Her manager had let him in? "Get out."

He'd leaned back against the doorway, his gaze moving over her so slowly, so assessingly, she'd had to fight the urge to pull the edges of her blouse together. "After I give you my proposition, *Kate*."

She should have walked to the door then and had him thrown out, but she'd been afraid of him.

"You've rejected my requests to join me for a drink three nights in a row," he'd murmured, eyes glittering as he pushed away from the door and walked toward her. "I figured I'd try another strategy." She'd backed up until her behind was against the dressing table, trying hard not to show her fear. "I know you're a student, Kate. I'm offering you fifty thousand dollars for a night. Any hard limits, I'll respect them."

She had stared at him, shocked. Shocked that anyone would pay that much for a night with someone. Shocked that that person would be *her*. She was the woman men shoved money at in a dirty, covetous thrill. Not a high-priced escort.

For a second, for one split second, it had crossed her mind that fifty thousand dollars would cover her tuition and living expenses for the year. She could spend the days going to school and studying like a normal student. She wouldn't have to be exhausted all the time turning her nights and days upside down…snatching a couple hours' study before she passed out at night. She could leave the backbreaking pain of her four-inch heels behind. Just like that.

Then hot shame had flooded through her. *How could she even be considering it?*

She'd pointed to the door. "Get the hell out of my dressing room."

He'd just stood there. "Everyone has a price, Kate. Name it."

"That's where you're wrong." She'd walked past him to the door and flung it open. "I don't."

He must have seen the hatred burning in her eyes, because he'd left. Afterward, Bruno had denied involvement, then had been fired a few weeks later for stealing money from the club.

Alexander Gagnon had shown up for the next two nights to see if she'd changed her mind. It had been the hardest two nights of her working career, her ability to concentrate nonexistent.

"Bailey?"

Davide was frowning, eyeing her plate. "You didn't enjoy your meal?"

She looked up to see the waitstaff hovering by her side, ready to remove the seafood salad sitting practically untouched in front of her. "I'm so sorry," she murmured. "I'm just a little off."

"Perhaps you got too much sun today," he suggested in French. "You are so fair."

"Perhaps," she agreed. "I'm sure I'll be fine after a good night's sleep."

Jared hadn't taken his eyes off her the entire meal. It could have been because she didn't seem able to add any intelligent insights to the conversation, or alternatively, *ask* any valuable questions. Either way, it felt hard to breathe and she needed to escape.

She excused herself and made a beeline for the ladies' room. It was downstairs, off the opulent drawing room, done in royal-blue marble with gold accents. She pulled in some deep breaths, splashed water on her ashen face, then pressed one of the thick, luxurious hand towels to her face.

Could a nightmare actually come to life? Because this was hers...

She applied some lipstick and pinched her cheeks to give them color, but she still looked deathly pale as she left her sanctuary and headed back upstairs. She had just stepped on deck when Alexander cut her off at the pass.

"You've done well for yourself, Bailey." He leaned his arm on the railing and blocked the way back to the others. "Or should I say Kate? What *is* your real name?"

Bailey gave him a blank look, fighting to keep her composure. "I'm afraid I have no idea what you're talking about."

"You think I don't remember you?" He rested his gaze on her face, as chilling and unnerving as it had been that night he'd sat in the audience watching her. "I remember every curve, every dip of your mind-blowing body. How you seduced every man in that room and left them begging for more."

A fresh wave of perspiration broke out on her brow. "You have the wrong woman," she rasped. "And this is not at all appropriate."

"I don't think I do." He pushed away from the railing and took the last couple of steps toward her. Bailey's heart knocked against her ribs. A cool Mediterranean breeze flitted over her but she felt vaguely feverish. "I saw it on your face that night. You wanted to say yes."

"I don't know you," she bit out and started to brush by him. He curled his fingers around her arm and brought her to a halt.

"They don't know, do they?" His smoky gaze heated with challenge. "You've moved on. Gone to a great deal of trouble to put your past behind you…"

Yes. And she wasn't going back there now.

"Get your hands off her, Gagnon."

Jared's low, menacing command came from behind them. She twisted around and found him watching them, hands clenched by his sides, tall, lean body coiled like a cat ready to pounce. Her heart zigzagged across her chest, threatening to explode right out of it. *God, no. He couldn't know about this.*

Alexander lifted his hand from her arm and stepped back. "Cool your jets, Stone. We were just having a conversation."

Jared took a step closer until he was toe-to-toe with Alexander. "I don't particularly like the nature of it. And neither does Bailey from the looks of it. So perhaps we should all return to the table for dessert?"

Alexander stared him down, just for the fun of it, Bailey guessed semi-hysterically. Her airways seemed closed to oxygen. Alexander lifted his hands in the air. "Beautiful, isn't she? Can't blame you. Ask her about the sexy mole on her hip, Stone. It's quite something…or maybe you already know that?"

Bailey's heart sank into the deck. A trickle of perspiration rolled down her neck as Alexander turned and sauntered off. *He had not just said that.*

Jared's gaze moved over her face. It was the stillness, the absolute stillness about him that got to her. "What is he talking about, Bailey? And how do you know him?"

She shook her head, in full denial. "I don't know him." And that was true. She didn't know anything about him. *Except he was now the key player who would decide their fate in the biggest deal of her life. Of Jared's life.*

Jared stepped closer to her. "Then why are you white as a ghost? Why have you been off since the moment you saw him?"

Her brain swirled in a desperate attempt to make this go away. Heart thumping painfully hard against her chest, she looked up at him. "He is an obnoxious jerk who has mistaken me for someone else. I am not good with boats, Jared. Never have been. And I don't want to make it an issue for Davide, who has been kind enough to take us on this lovely sail. So I think we should get back to the others before he worries."

She brushed past him before he could stop her and headed back to the table where dessert was being served. Somehow she managed to spoon a few mouthfuls of the undoubtedly delicious chocolate mousse into her mouth. But she tasted nothing. How could she when the world felt as if it was unraveling around her?

Alexander's cool, unruffled composure across the table was utterly unnerving. As if they'd been trading old war stories rather than him throwing her past in her face.

The night thankfully ended an hour later when Davide, she figured, took pity on her and suggested they do a final nightcap back at the villa. He insisted she rest rather than join them, and Bailey didn't protest. She brushed off Jared's intention to walk her to her room. "I'm fine."

He came anyway, wearing a frown.

"I'll be back to check on you," he said when they'd reached her room, planting a hand against the wall and looking her over. "Are you sure you're okay?"

"I'm fine." She pressed a hand to her pounding head, which was making her feel distinctly nauseous now. "Don't bother. I'll be asleep."

He stared her down. "I'll be back in half an hour."

Bailey forced some painkillers down her throat with a glass of water and paced her beautiful, airy suite. The more she paced, the more her head pounded. The two lives she'd so carefully kept light-years apart for so long had just crashed together with debilitating consequences. And the chances she was going to be able to keep them apart any longer were slim. Alexander Gagnon had offered her fifty thousand dollars to sleep with him almost ten years ago. And now she had to face him, *to pitch to him* over a boardroom table?

What if she had to work with him afterward?

The trails of perspiration rolling down her nape made her feel hot, feverish. She had not spent years of her life building her reputation in the business world to let a man like Alexander Gagnon destroy it. To assume he knew what she was when she wasn't anything like that.

I remember every curve, every dip of your mind-blowing body. How you seduced every man in that room and left them begging for more...

Alexander's words, cutting, accusatory, washed over her. Suddenly she felt dirty, so dirty. Hands shaking, she ripped off her jeans and tops. Found her bathing suit, threw it on and took the back stairs to the beach. The sea was dark and strewn with moonlight. The surf was up, eating into the sand with swift currents. She ignored how the darkness made it look dangerous, walked into it and struck out to a place unknown. To a place where the past couldn't find her.

Jared knocked on Bailey's door forty-five minutes later. He'd nursed a final brandy with Davide and the others, fought the urge to put his fist through Alexander Gagnon's face and ultimately restrained himself. He didn't believe Bailey for a second when she'd said she didn't know him. She'd had a violent reaction the minute she'd seen him. He'd *felt* it.

They don't know, do they? You've moved on. Gone to a great deal of trouble to put your past behind you.

What had Gagnon been talking about?

He knocked again on the door, his mouth tightening. *Nothing*. He waited five more seconds, knocked again and turned the knob. The door was open, a table lamp flooding the drawing room with light. No Bailey. He strode across the room, pushed her bedroom door open and saw the bed hadn't been touched. Her clothes were lying in a heap on the floor, which raised his antennae because Bailey was obsessively, compulsively neat.

He walked out onto the floodlit terrace and found it empty. Scanning the grounds, he searched for her. On the beach below a flash of white in the water caught his eye. Bailey's pale skin in the moonlight. *There.* He stripped off his shoes and socks and went after her.

She was so far out in the waves, he almost dived in fully clothed. But her pace was steady and her strokes sure, so he waited her out instead, his heels sinking into the sand. When she reached shore, she headed toward her towel, not fifteen feet from him, but she didn't notice him at all.

He allowed himself to enjoy the view while she toweled off. He'd had his fair share of women in his life. Some would say gone through them much more carelessly than a man should. But he'd never seen a woman look so utterly…goddess-like in a bathing suit.

The spotlights on the beach rendered those never-ending legs of hers a work of art. The product of gently rolling hips, they were slim enough to look delicate, curved enough to be irresistible. His hungry gaze moved upward, over her slim waist and more than ample chest, the perfection of which made his mouth go dry. She might not be a D cup, but she was exquisite.

She reached up and pulled her hair back into a ponytail, squeezing the water from it. It threw her delicate, unforgettable beauty into perfect spotlight. She looked untouchable…*haunted*.

It reminded him why he was here. He started toward her. She bent over to dry her calves. Her mouthwatering backside was not something to be missed. The round, dark mark on the curve of her buttock wasn't either. He froze. It was unmistakably a mole. A mole Alexander Gagnon knew intimately enough to call out.

He was across the sand and in her face so fast it made

his own head spin. Bailey looked up, her pale face catching the moonlight. Her hands slapped the towel around her hips but he was faster, spinning her around and pointing at the mark.

"You lied to me," he snarled. "You don't know him but he knows about intimate marks on your body? What exactly is going on?"

She tried to twist out of his hold, but he was stronger, his fingers digging into her upper arms. Her eyes flashed dark, almost gray in the moonlight, contrasting with her chalk-white cheeks. "Get your hands off me, Jared. Or are you no better than him?"

He let her go then, fury singeing his nerve endings. "We are negotiating a deal worth tens of millions of dollars a year, Bailey. I want the truth and I want it *now*."

She took a step back. Wrapped her arms around herself. "I told you the truth. I don't *know* him. I met him once when I lived in Vegas. He came on to me, I turned him down. That's it."

"That's it?" He slapped his palms against his temples, biting out a curse. Seconds passed, three, maybe four. Then he pinned his gaze on her face. "How did he know about the mole if you turned him down?"

She went even paler. "There's nothing further you need to know that has anything to do with this deal." Her chin came up. "That's all I'm answering and this conversation is done."

His blood fired. Raced in his veins. And he realized his fury had nothing to do with the deal. He wanted to know why that snake had an intimate knowledge of Bailey's behind. "I don't think so." He took a step closer, and this time she didn't back up. She stood her ground, eyes flashing. "You turn every man in Silicon Valley down. You act like you are untouchable…and yet that arrogant jerk, *known for his womanizing*, has had his hands on you… I don't get it."

She stepped up to him, her heat fusing with his until they were in danger of a spontaneous combustion. "What's the matter, Jared? You can't stand that it wasn't you? That Mr. Manifesto has met his match?"

He raked his gaze over her. "You know what, Bailey? You're right. I can't. Because if it had been me, you wouldn't have walked away."

She opened those luscious lips of hers to say something not very nice. He kissed her before she made it there. And by God, she was the sweetest female he'd ever tasted. Hot, honeyed perfection he savored for about two seconds before she raised her hand to slap him. He caught it in his and slid his other behind her nape, tangling it in her wet hair. Changed the kiss into a persuasive, seductive assault on her senses. The kind that always, without fail, worked.

Bailey wanted to fight but somewhere along the way, somewhere along the edges of the soul-destroying assault Jared was laying on her, she found escape. *Needed* it.

When he cupped the back of her head and angled her to take the kiss deeper, she let him. Moaned her approval when he brought his tongue into play and stroked her deeply. He smelled insanely good and he tasted better. Of cognac and expensive cigars. And she wanted more of him. A lot more.

He muttered something under his breath. Slid his hard thigh between her wet, shaking ones and brought her closer. So close his heart pounded beneath her palm. His hand at her back dragged her against his chest, urged her softness against his hardness. Her cool, air-tightened nipples brushed against him through the fine material of his shirt, and the heat that flooded her core came hot and hard. Like nothing she'd ever felt before.

He cursed again and dragged his mouth down the column of her throat, pressing openmouthed kisses against her damp skin. "Bailey," he breathed. "Who is he to you?"

Reality hit her like the hard slap of the night waves to her face. He wasn't kissing her because he wanted her. He was kissing her because he wanted to *possess* her. *Just like all the others.*

She sank a palm into his chest and pushed. Caught off guard, he stumbled backward. His gaze flew to hers. "What the—?"

"You are all dogs," she hissed, legs spread wide, feet planted in the sand. "Fighting over what you want. What you think is yours."

He gave her wild-eyed look a wary glance. "You were as into that kiss as I was."

Her elegant blond brows came together. "And now I'm walking away. *Again.* You were wrong, Jared. You aren't any different than the rest of them. You're all the same."

She left him standing there, staring after her, his jaw practically on the ground. Why was she always thinking Jared was different when he so categorically wasn't? Maybe *she* was the one losing her sense of judgment.

CHAPTER FIVE

JARED HAD RUN the path around the rocky beaches of the Cap for fifty minutes before he gave up trying to figure out what had happened last night and pulled up into a walk, sweat dripping from his chin. Given the lack of information coming from Bailey, the only thing that *was* clear was that Alexander Gagnon, Davide's heir apparent and the man who would own the decision as to whether to link Stone Industries and Maison Electronique in a five-year strategic partnership, knew his CMO intimately enough to call out a mole on her behind.

The thought had his already-pumping blood charging through his veins. He scowled and swiped his T-shirt over his face. Bailey had said she'd met Gagnon once, he'd propositioned her, and she'd turned him down. So how would he know about the mole? *And why, in God's name, was that a more pressing question for him than what he was going to do about the changing dynamics of this deal and the impact on his future?*

He let out a colorful curse and raked his T-shirt over his face again. Why wouldn't Bailey tell him the truth? What could be so horrible about her past that she couldn't tell him? That Alexander would call her on? He'd seen that look before, the one on Bailey's face last night. It was the exact same one his father had worn when the hounds had closed in. When his inability to escape had become inevitable—when all of his carefully constructed lies had started to unravel.

His chest tightened. He did not tolerate secrets. What he *should* do was march up there and tell Bailey she either came clean or she was out. There was too much riding on this pitch…this deal, not to have complete transparency. But the fact was, she was his ace in the hole. Davide loved her and her ideas. So eliminating her from the pitch was a nonstarter.

A massive bird of prey flew in from the sea, its wingspan at least eight or nine feet across. His gaze followed it as it arced and headed inland. A vulture? It reminded him of Alexander the way he'd tracked Bailey with his eyes last night. It had been beyond the look men had when they coveted something. It had been something else entirely…

He turned toward the house, his mouth twisting in a grimace. He'd been right from the beginning. The mystery that was Bailey had a history. A history that could blow the lid off this deal if he didn't find out what it was and defuse it. *Now.*

He made his way up the stairs toward their rooms, refusing to let himself address the other lethal ingredient flavoring the situation: the heat that had exploded between them last night. It was one thing to acknowledge an attraction. Another thing entirely to act on it. Because when the cat was out of the bag, it was all too easy to do it again.

Out of the question.

He let himself into his room, picked up his cell phone and dialed the PI he used to track his father, just to make sure he was alive, every now and again.

Danny Garrison picked up after almost seven rings with a sleepy, "'Lo?"

"I need you to dig up everything you can on my CMO, Bailey St. John."

There was a rustling sound in the background. "You do realize at some point I do go off the clock?"

He looked at his watch on the bedside table. Eight a.m. He hadn't even thought about the time difference. "Sorry. But I need this yesterday."

"Considering it *is* yesterday for me,, no problem." Sarcasm dripped from his PI's voice.

"Focus on her time in Vegas. She went to school there."

"Am I looking for anything in particular?"

Jared stared out at the cerulean-blue sky. At the vulture that had looped back over the seashore looking for breakfast.

"Something she'd want to hide."

Bailey shrugged out of an orchid-pink silk shirt, her third choice thus far, and tossed it on the bed. Nothing, *nothing* felt right about this presentation happening in thirty minutes. Nothing had since she'd laid eyes on Alexander Gagnon and realized it was *him*.

She snatched the pewter-gray version of the same shirt off a hanger and tugged it on. She needed to walk into that room today and nail the presentation. Forget the past and focus on the future. But her churning stomach wasn't cooperating.

Her hands fumbled as she pulled the shirt closed and did up the tiny pearl buttons. Would Alexander play nice? And if he didn't was she now playing Russian roulette with Jared's future? With this deal? Could she afford to do that? Should she just pull herself out now and accept the fact that her past had caught up with her? Do the right thing?

Her fingers tripped over the buttons, making her curse and focus her concentration. Surely Alexander had better things to do than focus on a bruised ego. He had a major directional partnership to consider for Maison. A company to take the helm of. He would be all business.

The knot in her stomach said differently.

Maybe Jared would fire her first for the inexcusable things she'd said and get it over with.

She shoved the last button through the slippery material with a vicious movement. How could she have kissed him? How could she have done that of all things? She didn't *feel* lust like that for men. Didn't let them close enough to even inspire it because her father had taught her that men were dangerous, unpredictable. Better avoided.

The arrival of their once-a-month welfare check had sent her father on his infamous benders like clockwork, typically ending with him trashing their house and whichever one of them had particularly annoyed him that day. Her mother had shielded them from him when she could, taking the punishment and sending her girls to the neighbors, but that had only made them feel worse when they'd arrived home the next day to a fresh set of bruises on their mother's face.

Add to that her experience as a dancer, and complete abstinence had been her solution.

A sharp knock on the connecting door brought her head around. She tucked a stray hair back in her chignon, turned and walked over to open it. Storm cloud Jared was in attendance today, his blue eyes crackling with electricity. *All business.*

"You ready?"

She nodded. "Let me get my notes."

Her prep stuff was in a pile on the desk. She'd left the notes on top, ready to grab, but last night in her agitation she'd thrown another pile on there and they didn't seem to be anywhere as she riffled through them, flicking pages upside down.

"Bailey." She hadn't realized he'd moved until he was beside her, his hand closing over hers. She looked up at him, teeth tugging at her bottom lip.

"They're right here, I just can't—"

"*Bailey.*" He took the papers out of her hands and put them down on the desk. "Tell me what's bothering you. Who is Alexander Gagnon to you? We are *partners* in this. I need to know what's wrong so we can handle it together."

She brought her back teeth together before she blew this entirely and pulled her hand free to continue searching for the notes. "He is nothing to me. I told you that."

"Then why are you a total disaster?"

"I am *not* a disaster." She rounded on him fiercely, eyes flashing. "This is personal, Jared, and I won't have it brought into this."

His mouth twisted. "Were you there last night? Because I was. Alexander is now the deciding voice in this deal. He did not take his eyes off you all night and then he followed you to the washroom where he was extremely confrontational. So don't tell me it's *nothing*, Bailey. He is an issue. And I won't have it affecting this deal."

She sank her hands into her hips. "Then pull me out."

"*I can't pull you out.* Davide adores you. He loves your thinking."

She pressed her lips together mutinously. She would rather *die* than tell Jared she'd been a stripper. A man who thought so little of women he'd written a manifesto about their place being in the bedroom. She could only *imagine* how derogatory he'd be. It made her stomach curl. As did the thought that he wouldn't want her anywhere near this deal.

He let out a muttered oath, his gaze on her face. "Tell me it wasn't something illegal. Whatever it is you're hiding."

Illegal? She stared at him in disbelief. *What the?* The flare of anxiety in his eyes, the frown furrowing his brow, made it hit home. His father. Of course he would be afraid of scandal.... Her stomach lurched dangerously.

She wanted to tell him, to reassure him it had everything to do with her, but she could not.

She put her hand on his arm, her gaze imploring him. "It's nothing like that. It's a personal matter Jared, that's all. You need to trust me on this."

He stared at her long and hard. As if he wasn't sure what to do with her. Then he let out a long breath. "Okay, this is how we're going to play it. We are going to walk into that room, blow them away with our ideas and win this contract. You are not going to be distracted. You are not going to address Alexander in any way, shape or form unless he asks you a question. Play to Davide, play to the other two. But do not let Alexander shake you."

Relief flooded through her. He wasn't going to push her. She could have kissed him except that had been a bad idea. "Got it," she said firmly. "You can trust me."

His gaze singed hers. "Too bad that doesn't go both ways."

She shook her head. "It does, I swear it. This is just… different."

The furrow in his brow deepened. "Someone's done a number on you, Bailey."

How about her life? Did that count?

He made a rough sound in his throat. "We have ten minutes. We should go set up."

She nodded and found her notes.

If Jared had expected Bailey to be shaky and off her game in the presentation, he was proven wrong. Something switched on in her brain when she walked into that room. Her survival instincts, he figured. She plowed through her slides with a steely determination and enthusiasm that made everyone at the table catch the spirit and engage. He watched that sharp brain of hers ignite, gather momentum as she fed off the feedback she was getting from the table and push her ideas to an even higher creative level. Not once did she look at Alexander, except to answer his pointed and often challenging questions.

His own strategies had been solid, but they had been lacking the marketing savvy Bailey possessed. Together they made a formidable team.

Don't fight the exodus from retail, she was counseling now, pointing at the screen. Touch consumers where they work and play, *show* them what they are missing in a lifestyle setting like a yoga studio that drives it home for them, then *sell* to them on the spot with the kiosks.

"Intriguing," Alexander conceded, "if a bit sacrilegious to a retailer like me. You're asking us to focus our marketing budget *outside* of the stores?"

"Some of it, yes," Bailey said, nodding. "It's a reality that people are moving away from brick-and-mortar retail to the online space. You need to get ahead of the trend now."

Alexander got to his feet and started pacing the room, a technique Jared figured he used to intimidate. "Yoga is niche, however. How is this really going to impact our bottom line?"

"You replicate it." Bailey flipped to her next slide. "You train demo staff, send them not just to yoga studios, but to running centers, health and wellness clinics, gyms… You seed the instructors first, make them fall in love with the product, and then you capture their students."

Alexander didn't look convinced. Bailey plunged on, undeterred. When she'd finished the last of the slides and Jared had closed with a "why Stone Industries" recap, they wrapped the presentation.

Davide looked at his son. "What do you think?"

"I like it," Alexander said, nodding. "I think the direct-to-consumer ideas are the strongest, they fit with our strategy, our target markets, but I am skeptical they can be rolled out on a large scale. And," he added, dropping a file folder on the table in front of Jared, "I *am* worried from this latest consumer research that you've alienated the target female consumer with your manifesto. You've dropped ten points in intent to buy with females since it happened."

Jared eyed the file in disbelief. "They'll be back up by next week. This is a flash in the pan." *And you know it.*

"Perhaps." Gagnon lifted a brow. "But the fact remains, the female demographic is our most important to capture right now. We can't afford to partner with a company that's alienated the market segment."

"It won't last," Jared repeated on a low growl.

"Likely not," Alexander agreed. "Your ideas are creative and sound. But I'm afraid I'm going to need market research to buy into them. So we're not all having a little enthusiasm party here that isn't based on reality."

Jared folded his hands in front of him, struggling to control his anger. "That will take time." He had a board meeting in two weeks he needed this deal signed, sealed and delivered for if he wanted to maintain control of his company.

Alexander shrugged. "We'd like you to repitch next week in Paris." He lifted a brow. "You're a busy man. If you have other engagements, send Bailey back to Paris with me. I can weigh in with what I know works and we can chew away at it."

Bailey turned gray. Jared's blood heated to a dangerous level. So *this* was Alexander's game? Taking care of unfinished business with Bailey? *Whatever that was...*

He looked at Davide but the Frenchman's expression was one of deference to his son. And Jared had nothing to work with but a botched attempt at humor instigated by a slightly wounded heart and a massive complication between his CMO and Maison's soon-to-be CEO.

He gathered the papers in front of him together with

a viciously efficient movement, refusing to let the fury simmering in his veins find an outlet. "That's very kind of you. But I have a friend with a villa on the outskirts of Nice. Bailey and I will regroup there, flesh the ideas out, and we'll present in Paris."

"I should add," Davide interjected, "that Alexander has indicated he'd like to hear from Gehrig Electronics as well."

Jared felt the earth tilt beneath his feet. "You're adding another company to the mix?"

Davide nodded. "We feel we need to do due diligence given some product launches we've been made aware of."

Due diligence. Jared felt the fumes rise off him. Gehrig hadn't been a factor until Alexander Gagnon arrived on the scene. His gaze flickered to Davide's son, sitting with his elbow on the table, jaw resting in his palm as he watched Jared with the intense interest of a hawk studying its prey. Davide had been right. His son liked to win. Except this had nothing to do with business and everything to do with Bailey.

Frustration clawed at him like a knife. He needed to be back in the States massaging an antsy board. But unless he wanted to muddy the waters with everything he *didn't* know, make accusations he wasn't sure of, he had no choice but to play along.

He forced what he was sure was a poor representation of a smile to his lips and stood up. "We totally understand. No problem, gentlemen. Let the best candidate win."

They answered a few more questions from the marketing team and made arrangements to pitch in Paris the week after. Then he and Bailey left to pack.

She stopped him outside their rooms, her hand on his arm, her face devoid of color. "I'm so sorry, Jared. This is my fault. I should have taken myself out of the deal."

He lifted his head. "You heard his reasons. He thinks I've alienated the female demographic."

"Yes, but—" She hesitated, worrying her lip between her teeth.

"He's playing games, yes," he growled. "We will talk more in Nice. *Much more,* Bailey. But if he wants to make this personal? Let him. I don't intend to lose."

CHAPTER SIX

By day three in Nice, Jared was feeling good about the progress they'd made on the presentation. They were holed up in a villa in the hills overlooking the sea owned by one of his friends, where the outside world was a distant distraction and pretty much everything else could wait.

Bailey had been in charge of scaling the creative ideas and adding in the market research data Alexander had requested. Which had, thankfully, proved them extremely viable. Jared concentrated on countering the intent-to-purchase consumer data Alexander had magically come up with, while also carrying out a full analysis of their competition, Gehrig Electronics, to uncover weak spots they could exploit. Unfortunately, Gehrig was a strong prospect with a rich technological heritage, a company going through a hot streak. And consumers loved buzz.

He tossed his pen down on Hans's desk. They would beat Gehrig, because although the other manufacturer had good products coming, he had better ones. Inspired ones that would set the world on fire. And although he'd had a whole strategic plan in place to unveil those products to the world, maybe it was time to let the cat out of the bag.

He got up and walked over to the window that overlooked the terrace. Bailey was sitting in a lounge chair in the sunshine, bent over her computer, hard at work as she had been for the past three fifteen-hour days. Invaluable to him. *And his ticking time bomb all in one beautiful package.*

She wasn't talking. She refused to address Alexander when he brought him up. It was a problem.

His mobile pealed from the corner of the desk. He walked over and retrieved it. Sam Walters. *Great.*

"Sam." He cradled the phone to his ear as he sat down and swung his feet up onto the desk.

"You didn't call. What's going on with Maison? I'm getting all sorts of questions I can't answer."

Join the crowd. His jaw came together with a resounding crunch. "Davide's passed the decision to his son, Alexander, who will become CEO next year. Alexander has decided he needs to do due diligence and give Gehrig Electronics a shot at the partnership. We're revamping the presentation to pitch against them next week."

"*Gehrig?* I thought this was a one-horse race?"

"Not anymore. Apparently my manifesto has dropped our brand rating with female consumers."

There was a long pause. Jared sighed. "Don't say it, Sam."

"You know I have to…the next time you get inspired to philosophize, Jared…*don't.*"

His lips twisted. "I would heartily agree with you, but that horse is out of the gate. Now we have to win."

"Yes, you do. You know I'm doing everything I can to shore things up for you until you get those products to market. But this will make a statement."

The muscles in his head clenched like a vise, a deep throb radiating through his skull. "I'm ultra-clear on this, Sam. Mea culpa, my mess. We will win. Meanwhile, let me know if you've got anything on Gehrig. I have a week to pull them apart."

"I'll make some calls."

"Thanks. Appreciate it."

"Jared?"

"Mmm?"

"You created Stone Industries. You're the only man who should be leading it. That's all the focus you need."

A smile curved his lips. "Thanks for having my back, Sam."

He put the phone down. Wondered what he would have done if he hadn't bumped into Sam at a start-up conference in the Valley and begun a lifelong friendship with the mentor who'd taken him under his wing when his father had gone AWOL. Who'd taught him that sometimes you *could* trust a person, that sometimes they *were* always there for you. And for a young, hotheaded Jared with an astronomically successful start-up on his hands, it had meant the difference between being a dot-com failure and the solid, profitable company Stone Industries was today.

An email brought his attention back to his computer screen. It was from his PI, Danny.

Bingo. Can I say, this one was my pleasure?

Why that made his insides twist, he didn't know. He opened the report, printed it and threw it in a folder. He also didn't know why he did that. Maybe he wanted to give Bailey a chance to tell him herself first. Maybe as he'd said from the beginning, trust was paramount to him. And maybe he knew what it was like to avoid the past because it only brought pain with it. And you couldn't change it no matter how much you wanted to.

Maybe he liked Bailey St. John far more than he was willing to admit.

Bailey was bleary-eyed by the time she dragged herself away from her computer to join Jared for dinner on the intimate little seaside terrace of the villa that overlooked the Mediterranean Sea. Smaller and cozier than Davide

Gagnon's showpiece of a home, it was luxurious but understated. The kind of place you could hide away forever in.

If only she could.

She pushed her hair away from her face and took a long sip of the full-bodied red Jared had unearthed from the cellar. You didn't actually relax when your boss looked as if he wanted to toss you off the cliff you were sitting on into the glorious azure water below. When decisions you'd made in the past suddenly seemed questionable when at the time, they'd seemed like the only way out.

Jared topped up her glass and stood up. "We're taking a break from work tonight. Both our brains are fried."

True. She stifled a surge of relief as she surveyed him in jeans and a navy T-shirt. Then thought maybe it was a bad idea because work had meant there was no space in her brain to remember *that kiss*.

"I think I might try to get some sleep," she demurred. "I haven't been doing so much of that."

He stared her down. "I built a fire in the pit. Sky's perfect for star spotting."

"And here I did not figure you for a Boy Scout."

"The wood was there," he said drily. "I piled it up. Come."

He picked up his glass and a blue folder he'd left on the chair and started walking down the hill. Hadn't he said no business? Maybe there was a detail he wanted to chew over, and that was good because then they wouldn't be diverging into the personal and Jared wouldn't be prying for information on Alexander Gagnon.

She stood up and followed him down to the fire pit with her wine. A series of big boulders with flat surfaces had been positioned around the pit to sit on. She lowered herself on one and watched as Jared lit the paper and coaxed the fire into a steady flame. "My father loved fires," he said. "Used to see how big he could make them go."

"How old were you when your father embezzled the money?"

He glanced at her, his profile hard and unyielding in the firelight. "More questions while you remain a mystery?"

She lifted a shoulder. "You brought him up."

"I was in my second year of university."

"That's why you dropped out?"

"Yes." He walked around and agitated the logs with a stick. "My parents had been helping me. I couldn't afford it after we lost everything."

"What happened to your father when it was discovered he took the money?"

He put the stick down and came to sit beside her on a neighboring rock. "He went to jail for three years."

Oh. She'd wondered if the more lenient laws on white-collar crime had kept him out of jail. "What does he do now?"

He stretched his long legs out in front of him and looked into the fire. "While he was in jail, my mother divorced him and married the head of the European Central Bank. When my father got out, he disappeared. I had him traced to the Caribbean, where he's been living in a hut on the beach ever since."

Wow. She tried to digest it all. "Do you have any idea why he did it?"

His lip curled, emphasizing the rather dangerous-looking, twisting white scar that ran across it. "Why he stole money from his employer and his closest friends? I'd have to be a psychologist to diagnose, but it might have something to do with my mother. She bled him dry every day of his life. And it was still never enough."

She pulled in a breath. Well, there you go. When you had attitudes like his, they came from somewhere. "What do you mean, bled him dry?"

He looked back at the fire. "She didn't know when to

stop. My father made a fortune in investment banking, but you could tell in the later years, he was done. He needed a break. But she never let him back off. Their wealth defined her. When she couldn't flash the latest hundred-thousand-dollar Maserati in front of her friends, when my father failed to provide, she left." His jaw hardened as he turned to her. "And if you're going to ask what happened then, my father lost the plot completely. As in his mind."

She looked over at him in the silence that followed, as big as any she'd encountered. "Still? Is he still like that?"

He kept his gaze trained on the leaping flames. "I haven't talked to him in a long time. I don't know. I send him money every month and he takes it."

She stared at him. How hard that must have been. How much it must have hurt. His manifesto made so much sense to her all of a sudden.

"Not all women are like your mother, Jared. I'm not."

"See, here's where I'm having a problem with that, Bailey." His low, tight tone sent a frisson of warning dancing across her skin. "I don't even know who you are. I have a multimillion-dollar deal tangled up in a woman with a past that could bring it crashing down around us. And you won't talk."

She flinched. "I've told you all that's relevant."

"Now you're going to tell me the real story." He picked up the folder sitting beside him and waved it at her. "This is where it ends."

She stared at the folder, her heart speeding up. "What is that?"

"It's your past, Bailey. In one convenient little package."

He was holding it with his far hand, far enough out of her reach that she never could have gotten to it. But she realized that wasn't the exercise.

"Who did it?" she demanded quietly.

"My PI. And trust me when I say he didn't miss anything."

Her blood pounded in her veins. Suddenly she felt very, very light-headed. "Jared. I can't—"

"You can. I've just told you the whole sordid story of my family. Now it's your turn. I haven't read it, Bailey. This is your chance."

She watched with big eyes as he stood up, walked to the fire and threw the folder into the flames. It sparked and licked up the paper until it turned gray and curled in on itself. Just like her stomach.

He turned back to her and stuck his hands in his pockets.

"Who is Alexander Gagnon to you, Bailey? What does he have on you?"

The flames licking the folder engulfed the remainder in a fiery glow. His gesture wasn't lost on her. He was giving her a chance to tell her side of the story. To trust him as he'd trusted her from the beginning.

A clamminess invaded her palms, a by-product of her racing heart and the adrenaline surging through her. A million thoughts filled her head. But in the end it came down to the truth.

"I met Alexander Gagnon when he came to my show at the Red Room in Las Vegas."

"The *Red Room*? Isn't that a strip joint?"

"That's right." She met his gaze. "I was a high-class stripper, Jared. I made oodles of money taking off my clothes for men."

His Adam's apple bobbed as if he was going to say something. His lips pursed as words formed, then he stopped, stared at her and waved a hand. "Go on."

She let her lashes drift down over her eyes. "When I was seventeen, I snuck into Tampa with a girlfriend of mine. We were hanging out in the big city, loitering on the street with pretty much nothing in our pockets, when a girl came up to me, a dancer from the hottest nightclub in the city. She told me I should apply for a job there. That I could make good money."

She twisted her hands in her lap and stared down at them. "You have to understand we were dirt-poor, my family. My father was an alcoholic, was off the job more than he was on. My mother was doing all she could to make ends meet, but her hair salon wasn't bringing in much. So when that girl—when she told me how much money I could make dancing, I was flabbergasted. I had dance training. It was one of the few things I was able to do because the local teacher let me study without paying because she thought I had potential."

He blinked. "So you started stripping?"

She nodded. "I made more money in a week dancing than my mother made in a month cutting hair. I took it home, paid for things. But when my father found out what I was doing, he hit the roof." Her mouth turned down. "They weren't making ends meet. My sister had no clothes but my money was *dirty* money. So he kicked me out."

A frown creased his forehead. "How old were you?"

"Seventeen. And believe me," she said bitterly, "nothing was ever so good. My father was not a nice drunk."

His gaze darkened. "God, Bailey, you were a baby. How were you even allowed to be in a bar?

"I lied. Got a fake ID."

He sat down beside her, rested his elbows on his knees and pressed his hands to his temples. "So you move from Tampa to Vegas where you go to school? And you keep stripping?"

"I moved there *to* dance. To pay my way through school. The money is fantastic in Vegas if you know what you're doing. I danced at a couple of different clubs, learned the industry, then I landed a slot at the Red Room. Every girl wanted to work there. It was very burlesque in the way we did the shows, they had the most beautiful women, and it was where all the high rollers hung out. I made a ton of money, easily paid for school every year."

He scrunched his face up. "Didn't it bother you the way men looked at you?"

"Like I belonged in the *bedroom?*" She threw his words back at him with a lift of her chin. "It was a job, Jared. Like any other occupation. I went to work, made a lot of money and got out when I could."

"You took your clothes off in front of strangers. That is not a normal job."

Heat rose up inside of her, headed for the surface. "My body was all I *had*. That was it. My sister, Annabelle, is *still* in Lakeland, working a ten-dollar-an-hour job and dealing with an alcoholic husband of her own." She stared at him, her frustration bubbling over. "I had dreams, Jared. Just like you had. Except you had a brain and I had my body so I used it."

His gaze darkened. "You also have an incredibly sharp brain. Why didn't you use *it?*"

"I didn't know that." Frustration grabbed at her, tore at her composure. "As far as I was concerned, I was low-income trash from the swamp. And no one ever tried to convince me differently. Not my teachers, classmates, not the girls who wouldn't let me into their cliques… I was the poor Williams girl who was never going to amount to anything. Well, dammit, I *did*."

He rubbed his hands over his eyes. "St. John is not your real name?"

She shook her head. "I changed it when I left Vegas for California."

"Is Bailey your real name?"

"Yes. My mother named me after her favorite drink."

His eyes widened at that. He was silent for a long time,

head in his hands. When he finally looked up at her, his expression was bleak. "When you say high-end stripper, what does that mean?"

Did she do favors for her clients on the side? Something inside her retracted. Curled up before it could be killed off. Before she showed him exactly how much that hurt.

"You want to know if I slept with the men I danced for?"

"Yes," he answered harshly.

"Would it make any difference if I said yes?" *Would it make the stigma of what she'd been worse?*

"*Goddammit*, Bailey, answer the question."

"I danced," she said stonily, "and then I went home and studied. Nothing more. *Ever.*"

He let out a long breath. "Where does Alexander Gagnon fit in all this?"

She laced her hands together and stared into the hissing, sparking fire. "Every week at the Red Room, the owner would have his favorite dancer do a special number at the end of the night. You were the star attraction, wore fancy red lingerie, got tons of tips for it. That week, he chose me." She registered the speculative look on Jared's face and chose to ignore it. "Alexander came to the Red Room for the first time on a Tuesday night. He gave me a huge tip and asked me to have a drink with him. For some reason, I refused. He was well-dressed, had this aura about him you couldn't ignore, but there was something I didn't trust. And in that business it was all about instinct.

"He didn't want any of the other girls. He came back two other nights after that, always tipping heavily and asking me to have a drink with him. On the third night, I said no, went to my dressing room and started taking off my makeup. I was the last girl to leave. The others were all in a rush to go out that night and I was just going home to study so I took my time. At one point, I had this feeling I wasn't alone and I turned around and there he was—Alexander," she qualified. "Just standing there."

His gaze narrowed. "How did he get past the bouncers?"

She grimaced. "I found out later he'd bribed Bruno, my manager, to make them look the other way. I don't know what Alexander had on Bruno to make him do that—Bruno was a big gambler, he owed people a lot of money so maybe that was it. Anyway," she said, waving a hand, "I was shocked, totally thrown. I told him to get out. He completely ignored me."

"Then what?" Jared growled.

"He propositioned me."

"What do you mean propositioned you?"

"He offered me fifty thousand dollars to sleep with him."

A dangerous glimmer entered his eyes. "For one night?"

"Yes."

"What happened when you turned him down?"

Her fingers tightened around her glass. "He told me everyone has a price. To name mine. I told him to get the hell out again and this time he did."

"And that was it?"

"He came back two more nights to see if I'd changed my mind. I never saw him after that."

"Jesus—Bailey—" He stood up and paced to the fire. Raked his hands through his hair. "Why didn't you tell me?"

"Tell *you?*" She gave him a disbelieving look. "You, the man who just wrote a manifesto about how women belong in the bedroom, not the boardroom? You have to be joking."

"Oh for God's sake, you know that doesn't apply to you." He gave his head a shake. "What did he say to you on the yacht? You looked shaken."

"He realized that nobody knows. That I've hidden my past."

"And?"

She shook her head. "You interrupted us then."

His gaze sharpened on her face. "You can't run away from the past forever. It always catches up with you."

Her mouth twisted. "So I should just tell everyone I was a *stripper*? Get it out of the way? I have worked my *entire life* to put my past behind me, Jared. I'm not ashamed of what I did. But others will judge me. 'Jared Stone's chief marketing officer—former stripper.' How do you think that will go over?"

He was silent. Because she was right.

"He still wants you," he muttered after a long moment. "He wants to win. That much is clear."

Bailey felt her past close like a noose around her neck. Finally it had caught up with her. She'd always thought it might. But did it have to be *now*? Right at the moment she'd thought she just might rise above it?

Tears of frustration singed the back of her eyes. She drained the rest of her wine and set the glass on the ground. "I am now a liability," she said quietly. "You need to take me out of this presentation, Jared. Eliminate me from the equation. You know it and I know it."

Blue eyes tangled with darker blue. The flicker in his was almost indiscernible, but she didn't miss it. The acknowledgment that she was right.

"Pull me out," she repeated dully, getting to her feet. "It's the right thing to do."

And then she walked away before she bawled her eyes out.

Jared watched Bailey go, so dumbstruck by what she'd just told him he was actually incapable of pursuing. *She'd been a high-end stripper in Vegas. She had taken her clothes off for total strangers every night, pocketed scads of money and put herself through school with it.*

The idea of *Bailey* putting herself on display like that, letting men drool over her like that, was so far-fetched it was almost laughable. He would have laughed if he wasn't so appalled. Here he'd been picturing her *selling shoes* at the local mall to put herself through school. *Making cappuccinos at the local café*…instead she'd been balling up the cash men shoved in her G-string to survive and sacrificing her innocence along with it.

Dear God. And then there was the image of Bailey dancing in expensive lingerie on a stage that wouldn't leave his head…how many men had gotten off seeing her like that? And why did that idea *torture* him?

He went for the whiskey then, because quite honestly, he didn't know what else to do. A sixteen-year-old Lagavulin he found in the lounge would do the trick. Might help wipe from his head the look on Bailey's face when he'd tossed that file into the fire and forced her hand.

She'd never wanted anyone to know about that part of her life. And he'd made her reveal it.

He carried the tumbler out onto the terrace and rested his palms on the railing. The sea glistened at the base of the cliffs in the moonlight. The whiskey slid down his throat, smoky and salty, a welcome heat to counter the disquiet plaguing him. He'd needed to know. *Had* to know. The ends justified the means. But now what?

He should take Bailey off the pitch. He should handle it alone for both their sakes. It was clear Alexander Gagnon had a fixation with her. He'd offered her an insane amount of money to sleep with him. And a man like that just didn't give up…he pursued until he won. To hell with his deal.

But there was also Davide to consider. Bailey was his ace in the hole when it came to the elder Gagnon, and he was still very much in the picture. He needed her thinking to win.

The whiskey slid down his throat, smooth and fiery. Bailey's words echoed in his head.

I had dreams, Jared. Just like you had. Except you had a brain and I had my body so I used it.

The look on her face when she'd given up...when she'd told him to take her off the deal.

His guts twisted. Bailey had fought her way out of a life most people would have accepted as their fate and never tried to rise above. But she had. She hadn't let it define her. She was the smartest, most composed, drop-dead beautiful woman he'd ever met. Her brilliant ideas had *made* their presentation.

He stared out at the brightly lit boats bobbing on the sea, their smooth roll telegraphing a calm night to come. And a strange kind of certainty settled over him. Bailey needed someone to believe in her. He was pretty sure she'd never had that. And he wasn't giving up on her.

It wasn't even a question.

It was then that Jared Stone realized his manifesto was the biggest piece of crap he'd ever written.

Bailey had just slipped her nightie on when a knock came at the door. Her emotions far too close to the surface, she stayed where she was.

"I'm fine, Jared. I'm good with all of it. I just need some sleep."

"I'm not leaving until I talk to you. Open the door."

His tone was hard; implacable, like Jared was. She cursed, grabbed her robe and tugged it on. Attempted to compose herself as she pulled the door open and found him standing there like a fierce warrior, filling the doorway with his broad-shouldered frame.

"I am not dropping you," he announced. "We are partners and we are doing this together."

"Jared—" She bit her lip, furiously blinking back tears.

Even after what she'd just told him, he was still backing her?

"We are a team," he said quietly, blue gaze softening. "I've told you that from the beginning. You trusted me enough to tell me about your past tonight and I know that wasn't easy. I *need* you in that room with me, Bailey. You've proven that."

A tear slid down her cheek. She couldn't help it. No one had ever shown such faith in her. She'd been going it alone since she was seventeen and suddenly, she felt so tired of it. Tired of fighting every battle by herself.

"Christ, Bailey." He took a step forward and brushed the tear away with the pad of his thumb. "Did you think I was just going to abandon you? After everything you've put into this? Those are *your* ideas Davide loves."

She looked down, anywhere but at him, but the tears kept rolling. "I thought you wouldn't respect me, that you wouldn't want me anywhere near this deal if you knew what I'd been…"

He slid his fingers under her chin and brought her gaze back up to his. "I am not going in there without you. And as for respecting you? I've never respected a woman more in my life. For who you are. For what you've done…"

Something melted inside of Bailey. Something that had been frozen for so long she'd forgotten it existed. She thought it might be her heart.

"But what about Alexander? Lord knows what he's capable of and I would never forgive myself if you lose this deal because of me."

"I'm not going to lose," he said softly. "Alexander Gagnon likes to win. I like to win more."

"But—"

He pressed his fingers against her lips. She fell silent in a sea of confusion that had only one focal point: the electricity that was so strong between them that it held her completely still as his eyes darkened with an emotion she couldn't read. He put his mouth to the hot, wet tears dampening her cheeks and kissed each one away with a slow drag of his lips that started out comforting and ended up something else entirely.

Hot. Scorching hot.

She didn't know who kissed who first. It was unspoken communication, her hands cupping his jaw, devouring him, while his found the belt to her robe, untied it and pushed it off her shoulders. She moved into him until her bare skin was molded against the hard muscles of his chest, tasting him, knowing him, until she wasn't sure where she started and he ended.

"You are so beautiful," he rasped, his mouth leaving hers to trail a path of fire down her throat. When he hit the ultrasensitive spot between her neck and shoulder, she gasped and arched to give him better access. He took full advantage, nuzzling and exploring until she dug her hands into his shoulders and demanded more.

He drew back and took her in. Color swept every centimeter of her skin. "We can't do this. You are my boss."

He shook his head. "It's never been that simple with us and you know it."

"Jared…"

He slid a finger underneath the spaghetti strap of her nightie and slipped it off her shoulder. Her heart pounded in her chest as he weighed her breast in his palm and learned the shape of her. She could have pulled away then, *should* have pulled away, but the want in her shocked her, the fact she'd never let a man touch her like this becoming inconsequential somewhere around the time he took her inside the heat of his mouth and her knees went weak.

The rush, the sweet, all-encompassing rush knocked her brain sideways. She buried her fingers in his hair and closed her eyes. And for once in her life just let herself feel. *Want*. He slid his jean-clad leg between her thighs and brought her closer. He was hard and rough against her sensitive skin and it excited her beyond belief.

She moved against him and whimpered. "Jared…"

He slid the strap off her other shoulder and flicked his tongue over her engorged nipple. Gave her what her husky entreaty hadn't been able to verbalize. And the unfamiliar throb inside her reached a fever pitch.

Somehow she was in his arms and he was striding across the room to the sofa in the lounge. He sat down, wrapped her legs around him and brought his mouth back to hers in a red-hot kiss that pulled her under again.

She should have been alarmed at how fast things were moving, *that they were moving at all* given her lack of experience, but somehow with Jared, it felt so right. She buried her mouth in the hollow of his neck and explored his musky, salty, utterly male scent.

He found the hem of her nightie and pushed it up. Her gaze tracked his movements as he trailed his fingers over the concave dip where her hip met thigh.

"You are all woman," he murmured huskily.

"Too much, I'd say."

He shook his head. "You are perfection. You know what I was thinking that night you asked me to choose the shoes?"

"What?"

He trailed his fingers along the edge of her panties, down to where she was on fire for him. "This."

His whispered answer sent a shiver down her spine. Her stomach curled into a hard, tight ball as he brought his thumb to her center and rotated it so achingly slowly she thought she might go up in flames.

"I thought that if we'd been on a date," he continued huskily, "I would have kept you there until I'd made you come…at least twice."

She lost her composure then. "Jared—"

He put his fingers to her mouth. "Better late than never, don't you think?"

Having never had an orgasm in her life, Bailey couldn't answer that question. And good thing she didn't have to, because Jared flipped their positions then, went down on his knees in front of the sofa and lifted his gaze to hers.

"Spread your legs for me, sweetheart."

Her pulse went into overdrive, tattooing itself against her veins so hard she thought she might pass out. She didn't know it was possible to feel so turned on and so excruciatingly self-conscious at the same time, but the blazing heat of his deep blue gaze spurred her on. *Lustful. Full of want. Nothing she wasn't ready to give.*

Her thighs fell apart. He worked his palms up the inside of them, arranging her to his satisfaction until she couldn't look anymore and closed her eyes. And then his hands were under her hips, urging her forward; his mouth was hot against her center, burning a trail against her damp panties, and Bailey forgot her name.

He tugged off her underwear with an impatient movement, setting his mouth to her heated flesh, where she was wet and wanting him. Hot, sweet pleasure coursed through her, curled her toes.

"Beautiful, you are so beautiful," he murmured against her skin. "Twice might not be enough."

She closed her eyes. The hot slide of his tongue against her made her whimper. And he did it again and again, varying the pressure and rhythm, asking her how she liked it. She gave him rational, honest responses at first. And then she started shaking and needing something more and she begged him to shut up.

His soft laughter flickered across the sensitive skin of her thighs. The smooth slide of his finger as he eased it inside her tore a moan from her throat. Then he brought his tongue back into play and the world went a hazy gray. This, she realized instinctively, was what she needed.

"Bailey," he murmured, "baby. Give it up."

She arched her hips and clutched the fabric of the sofa as he increased his rhythm. She begged and he gave no quarter, adding another finger, increasing the intensity until she went over the edge, her palm against her mouth the only thing preventing her scream from tearing into the night.

When her body had stopped shaking like a leaf, her brain started to function again.

So that was what all the fuss was about.

Jared leaned forward and smoothed her hair back from her face. "What did you say?"

"Nothing." OMG had she just said that out loud?

He gave her a curious look, then a slow smile curved his lips as he rose to his feet, worked his palms beneath her and swung her up in his arms. "That was *one*."

Bailey's heart pounded with every step he took toward the gorgeous turquoise-blue bedroom. She had to tell him. *Now.*

"Jared." She poked a finger into his shoulder. "Stop for a second. I need to tell you something."

He halted midstride, his gaze flicking to her face. "What?"

Color rushed to her cheeks, rendering them a red-hot mess. "I've never—I mean you should know that I am a—"

The words died in her throat as he went as gray as she was red.

"You are goddamn joking."

CHAPTER SEVEN

THE LOOK ON Bailey's face sent a cold rush through Jared, like the mistral gone awry right up the center of him. He dropped her to the floor so fast she didn't have time to brace herself, and his hands at her waist were the only thing that held her up.

"Tell me you're joking," he repeated harshly.

She pushed a hand against his chest and stood back, her chin lifting to a defiant angle. "What's the big deal?"

His eyes rounded. "You're a twenty-nine-year-old, former stripper, *virgin?*"

Her face went even hotter. "Are you going to tag that description on every time you talk about me now? Because I'm afraid that doesn't work for me."

He closed his eyes and raked his hair back from his face. "I don't understand how this could happen."

Her mouth flattened. "Simple. I haven't gotten into bed with a man. Not that you'd understand anything about that. Half the women in the Valley are walking around with your cute little diamond charm bracelets on as if they were the Medal of Honor."

He let out a harsh breath and opened his eyes. "It was the combination of your age and background, Bailey. You haven't exactly been living in a nunnery."

She put her hands on her hips and stared at him. "What

were you hoping? That I'd have all sorts of tricks up my sleeve, *living the life?*"

His gaze narrowed. "I wasn't actually thinking, Bailey. As you can imagine after what just happened."

Taking her to bed and having her until sunrise had been the only thing in his head...no thinking involved there.

His mouth twisted in a scowl. Not happening now, that was for sure. Virgins wanted rings on their fingers. Assurances of undying love. That part of his manifesto hadn't been wrong.

"Why?" His frustrated, sexually aroused body wanted to know. "Why would you be twenty-nine and a virgin?"

She wrapped her arms around herself. "I dunno, Jared. I'd have to be a psychologist to say." His scowl grew as she tossed his words back at him. "I didn't date in Vegas. The men who asked me out were only after one thing, given my profession. They didn't exactly want to court me. Then when I came to the Valley I was just too busy working."

"And your father," he pointed out. "He can't have given you a very good picture of men to work with."

No. He'd broken her heart. Her mother's heart. *All of their hearts* again and again to match his own broken one. Twenty years of wanting to be the hero you once were.

She brushed her hair out of her face. "I'm sure that had something to do with it."

He frowned. "I don't buy that you were too busy to date in the Valley. I've seen the men pursue you."

"Because I'm a challenge," she pointed out. "You think I don't know what they say about me? The wagers they make? The minute I go to bed with one of them it's going to be all over the airwaves faster than your manifesto." She wrinkled her nose. "I'd rather not bother."

"So what was that?" He jerked his head toward the sofa. "You were all in there, Bailey."

"Stupid me." She rolled her eyes. "We do have this

chemistry, you and I. And for one second, *five minutes*," she amended sarcastically, "I was doing what I wanted. I wasn't holding back."

His heart stuttered. The urge to pick her up, walk into that bedroom and finish what they'd started made him shove his hands in his pockets. Because while he liked Bailey, might even be *fond* of her, despite the fact that he wanted to take her to bed more than he'd ever wanted a woman in his life, he didn't do the big *V*. Wasn't capable of it. It would be like asking him to vote Republican. To suggest he leave a big messy pile in the middle of his impeccably clean desk.

Clean desk, clean mind, his Zen master had told him on that thirty-day search to find his soul. If he slept with Bailey, there might never be enough meditation for that.

He lifted his gaze to her rather glazed one, resolute despite his screaming body. "I just have one question for you."

She gave him a wary look. "What?"

"Don't you ever get…*frustrated*?"

Her eyes darkened. "Get out of my room, Jared."

How were you supposed to greet the day when you'd just spent the night before getting down and dirty with your boss? It wasn't a particular skill Bailey had arrived in France with, and the thought of facing him across a plate of croissants while she remembered him on his knees between her thighs, *devouring* her, wasn't going to fly.

She yanked a pillow over her face and lay back in the big king-size bed. Her only saving grace was she hadn't screamed out loud. But even that was tempered by the fact that her moans of approval *had* been loud and clear. And *if* he'd taken her to bed, she would have let him take her virginity. She would have let *Jared Stone* take her virginity. Because for a moment there, she'd thought she'd seen the real Jared. The man behind the manifesto. The man who thought enough of her that he was backing her when he shouldn't be…

Who had called her the smartest marketing person he'd ever worked with.

I've never respected a woman more in my life. For who you are. For what you've done.

Ugh. She pressed the pillow harder against her face. Had he just been trying to get her into bed? Had he been intrigued by her past and wondering how hot she was? How skilled? But even as she thought it, she knew it wasn't right. Jared was risking too much standing behind her to just be out for sex. His Achilles' heel was his utter and complete inability to commit. This was right within character. A virgin must be an intensely scary, disconcerting phenomenon to him. *What had she expected him to do?*

She threw the pillow off, fury at herself coursing through her. He might respect her even after all she'd told him, but he was still Jared—a man no female should get anywhere near unless she was as shallow as he was when it came to the art of the casual hookup.

It made her wonder about the rest of the manifesto she hadn't read…

She swung her legs over the side of the bed, padded into the lounge and woke up her computer. Gave the scattered sofa pillows a grimace. His manifesto now had five million views. She typed in the word *virgin* and pressed Find. And there it was. Bolded.

Never, ever take a virgin home with you unless you're prepared to open up the homestead to her. Lock, stock and barrel. There is no "see how it goes" with a virgin. I've seen better men than me crash and burn. Hard.

Her vision misted over. What was wrong with her? When had she forgotten exactly who Jared was? *About the same time he had kissed her brain into some sort of ancient and useless artifact.* Because let's face it. Some women would trade their self-respect for that skill in the bedroom.

If she'd kept her mouth shut last night, she would have.

She got to her feet with a jerky movement, strode into the bathroom and pushed her obviously cloudy head under the hot spray of the shower. She was going to pretend last night had never happened. Appreciate what Jared was doing for her because he *was* risking a great deal by keeping her in this pitch, she knew that. And she was going to win it for him. Then she was going to get far away from Jared Stone while she still had her wits about her.

Jared was eating breakfast on the terrace when she arrived downstairs, newspaper spread out in front of him, undoubtedly having already inhaled a couple of the croissants from the basket as he did every morning. He had the highest metabolism of anyone she'd ever encountered, which she had to admit was likely stoked by all the *muscle* on display for her this morning. Athletic shorts and a gray T-shirt left little of it to the imagination.

Not helping.

Heat rushed to her face as he glanced up at her, and the night before slammed into her brain like an unavoidable fact. But this was cool and controlled Bailey in charge now. She could do this.

She sat down opposite him at the little table. His gaze traveled over her face. "Good morning."

She tried to ignore how sexy and rusty his voice sounded before he'd put it to use for the day and muttered a greeting back. Refused to imagine how superhot it would be if she was *still* in his bed at this time of the morning, which of course she was not, because he'd walked out on her as though she was a communicable disease.

Not that she was bitter about it or anything.

She reached for the croissants, still warm from the oven, her fingers closing over one with chocolate oozing out of it. "Georgina outdid herself this morning."

He gave the croissant a hard look. "I've been trying to figure out how they get the chocolate in the center."

"You roll them this way." She spread her napkin on the table and demonstrated.

He lifted a brow. "You're handy in the kitchen, too. That's a big turn-on."

Apparently not when combined with her virgin status. She picked up a knife and sliced through the croissant with a vicious movement. "But then I would want to commandeer all your baking supplies at the homestead. How horrific…"

A smile edged his lips. "I knew you were going to look that up. And actually, Bailey, I love nothing more than when a woman cooks for me. As long as she shuts the door after her when she leaves."

She closed her eyes against the oh-so-tempting vision of him with the chocolate pastry smeared all over his face.

"I don't know if I can do this."

"What? Live with me for another week?" His tone was overtly amused. "Feel free to speak openly."

She shook her head. *No. No thanks.* She was not letting him draw her in again. He was a professional instigator—head and shoulders more skilled than her in that department. She picked up the coffeepot, poured herself a cup of the steaming brew and set the tall silver canister back on the table so it effectively blocked him from view. He reached out and slid it aside, laughter dancing in his eyes. "You think you can block me out with a coffeepot?"

"Not really." She gave him an even look as she stirred milk into her coffee. "But what's the alternative? We talk about last night?"

He shrugged. "At least you had some sort of relief. Me? It took a five-mile run this morning to work it out."

Her already-hot face incinerated. "I am so not talking to you about this. In fact, I suggest we never reference it again."

A wide smile curved his lips. "Fine. I'm just saying you aren't the only cranky one this morning."

Her eyes widened. "I'm not cranky." Angry, more like it. "Reading the rest of your manifesto was a good wake-up call. Stupid me for thinking my virginity wouldn't make a difference to a Lothario like you."

His smile faded. "First, I think that's an exaggeration. And second, there's only one reason I walked away from you last night, Bailey. I don't make promises I can't keep. I don't like taking women for a ride like some guys do. And if that makes me a jerk then so be it."

"Who was asking you for a promise?" She shook her head in amazement. "You're so caught up in yourself, in what you *think* you know about people, you haven't got a clue, do you?"

He leaned forward and rested his elbows on the table, his gaze spearing hers. "Tell me you don't want the full deal. A man who loves you. A diamond ring…everything that goes with it."

She sank her teeth into her bottom lip, knowing he was sucking her in again but too stung to care. "You want the truth, Jared? I don't know what love is. I've never had it so how would I? My parents kicked me out when I was seventeen…dancing pretty much ruined my trust in men…" She lifted her shoulders. "I've been fighting my own battles for so long, I'd settle for a man who respects me. A man who tells me the truth." She angled her chin at him. "One who wants me for who I am."

His lips tightened. "This is about *my rules*, Bailey. Not you. If you hadn't been the last virgin on the face of the planet last night we'd be acting out my deepest, darkest fantasies about you—and believe me, I have many."

Her breath caught in her throat, heat searing through her in a potent combination of lust and humiliation. "You are such a jerk, you know that?" She pulled in a breath and stared at the hard, uncompromising lines of his face. "You know what I think? I think your rules are a cop-out. Your parents' marriage was a disaster so you think all relationships are like that. You avoid ties to anyone so you don't have to face the reality of being in one yourself." She lifted a brow. "I think you're scared."

His face took on a gray tinge. "Look who's talking."

"You're right." She abandoned her croissant and pushed away from the table. "But at least I admit it."

"Where are you going?" he barked. "We aren't finished here."

"I need a walk. All of this denial is making me lose my appetite."

Jared had been trying to avoid the truth the entire two hours he'd been up and Bailey had been in bed. Kissing her, touching her like that last night, had almost been an inevitability. He got that. *Bailey's being a virgin had not.* How did *anyone* reach the age of twenty-nine and be a virgin? Honestly?

He watched her walk down the path toward the beach, back ramrod straight, her shoulders up around her ears.

For once I wasn't holding back. For once I was doing what I wanted.

He scowled and tossed his napkin on the table. How was he supposed to interpret that? What was he supposed to *do* with that? He needed to stay away from Bailey. She was like a flashing neon danger sign for him. A weakness he couldn't afford to indulge at a time when winning this deal was all that mattered. So why was he now striding down the path after her like a raging bull intent on having his way?

She looked warily at him as he fell into step beside her. "Go away, Jared."

"When you said dancing destroyed your trust in men, what did you mean?"

She gave him a long look. "You wouldn't ask that if you'd spent any amount of time in a strip club."

He shrugged. "It's not my thing."

"I don't imagine. Not when the women are beating down your door for a night with the *lion*."

"Bailey…"

"Why are you asking this?"

"I want to know."

She looked as though she was going to tell him to mind his own business. He wasn't sure what was going on in those cool blue eyes. Embarrassment? The need to protect herself? But then she lifted her shoulders. "There are four types of men who come to a strip club. The jokers, the guys who come in with a bachelor party or to party with their friends, they drink too much, leave you nice tips and go on their way. Then there's the regulars. Some of them become friends, they pay you to dance for them, sit with them, listen to the things their wives won't because their marriage is so far gone, they don't listen to them at all anymore."

His mouth twisted. "You realize you're proving my point."

She ignored him. "Those are the good regulars. Who can become bad regulars if they fall for you. Then they decide you need to be rescued. That you shouldn't be living this life and they want to marry you. If you're unlucky, they become stalkers and then they're a real problem."

"Did that happen to you?"

"Once. The club saw him follow me to my car and called the police."

He looked horrified. "And the final kind?"

"The men who want to degrade you. The ones who are unsuccessful in life, feel they aren't appreciated enough at home—the ones who don't feel *manly* enough. They come in to put themselves on a power trip. They'll call you names, call you stupid, whatever makes them feel better about themselves by making *you* feel like you're about an inch tall."

"So how did you deal with that?" A wry smile curved his mouth. "I can't imagine you took it well."

"I didn't. One night when a guy grabbed my butt, I slapped him across the face." Her mouth pursed. "He hit me back, only, much harder."

Jared's heart lurched. "What happened after that?"

"The bouncers threw him out. He came back the next night."

"They let him back *in*?"

"He was spending. That's all they care about."

"Did that happen often?"

"No. It was more verbal abuse. You got used to it, you developed a thick skin, but it still wears away at your self-confidence."

She looked so vulnerable, so tiny beside him when some of those guys must have been twice her size, it made his skin burn just thinking about it.

"What were the rules on personal contact?"

Her gaze skipped away from his. "To make the really good money, you had to do private dances."

"Lap dances?"

"Yes."

He'd never had a lap dance. He'd watched his groom-to-be buddy have one and hadn't felt any desire to do that with a stranger. Hadn't seen the sexiness in it. His buddy had, though. He'd loved having the beautiful girl intimately plastered across his lap.

"Was this," he asked Bailey, his voice a little on the rough side, "all done with or without clothes?"

Rosy color stained her delicate cheekbones. "We had to wear bottoms. We wore two, in fact. I'm not even sure why. It might have been more of a fashion statement."

The thought of Bailey dressed like that, dancing on a guy's lap, had him asking, "Didn't it bother you, doing that?"

"Of course it bothered me," she snapped. "It wasn't Sunday school, Jared. It was a job—a very lucrative job where men paid me a lot of money to take off my clothes. And maybe if I hadn't had to worry about money my entire life, hadn't had to wear hand-me-downs every day to school, I would have chosen differently. But I didn't have that luxury and I wanted to make a better life for myself."

Point taken.

She looked out at the sea, the sun slanting over her alabaster skin. "Most of the men were fine. Most of them respected the line and didn't cross it."

"Except for the ones like Alexander."

She looked back at him, the remnants of a memory in her eyes. "Do you know what he said to me that night in my dressing room?"

He was pretty sure he didn't, but he nodded anyway.

"He said he would respect my hard limits."

Jared's hands clenched into fists by his sides. "You stay away from him in Paris," he said harshly. "I don't want you interacting with him."

She nodded. "I will."

He didn't want Gagnon anywhere near her. He was also sure he never wanted a man to raise a hand to her again. *Put* a hand on her. *Ever*.

He raked a hand through his hair and blinked against the sunshine breaking through the clouds as they stepped down onto the beach. Absorbed the uneasy feeling in his gut as he worried he was seriously losing his edge. Protecting Bailey against Alexander Gagnon was a given. The rest of it—the urge to keep her for himself—that was something he could never, ever do. He wasn't even sure where such a crazy thought had come from.

CHAPTER EIGHT

An UTTERLY BRILLIANT, rock-solid presentation under their belt, Jared and Bailey landed in Paris on Sunday night after a quick hour-and-a-half flight north from Nice in the Stone Industries jet. A car picked them up from the terminal and whisked them into the city, lights sparkling from every vantage point as dusk fell.

Jared studied the play of color across the Seine as they neared their hotel in the Left Bank, thinking the City of Light was so much more appropriate a descriptor than the City of Love. For one thing, he thought, mouth twisting, love was a myth perpetuated by all the romantics of the world. Secondly, there was no city as gorgeous as Paris at night.

He watched Bailey once again play twenty questions with their driver, asking him about the city landmarks.

I don't know what love is, she'd said. *I've never had it so how would I? I'd settle for a man who respects me. A man who tells me the truth. One who wants me for who I am.*

He pursed his lips and stared out at the elegant facades of the historic buildings that lined the river. Bailey was everything a man in his right mind would want in a woman. Intelligent, stunningly beautiful, interesting and desirable... How had one not snapped her up, pushed his way past that impenetrable facade? Tapped into that wistfulness she kept hidden so well? Had the life she'd led made her bury it that deep?

He put it out of his head as the car whipped around a corner and pulled to a halt in front of their elegant old hotel. It was exactly that vulnerability, the fact that she was untouched, that was going to keep him a hundred paces from her at all times if he knew what was good for him.

Their takeoff spot had been delayed in Nice, which meant they had less than an hour before they were due at the dinner that had been organized for them and their Gehrig counterparts. Enough time to check in to their hotel, change and go. Jared left Bailey to shower and dress in the suite that adjoined his and did the same.

He had showered and was pulling on his shirt when a knock came at the connecting door. He strode over and pulled it open, finding a fully dressed, toe-tapping Bailey on the other side. Her gaze moved over his chest, down over the muscles of his abdomen in a caught-off-guard perusal that couldn't be mistaken for anything but total appreciation.

It made his vow to avoid anything that constituted lust between them snag in his throat.

"I just need a tie," he muttered, turning around and putting distance between them.

Bailey walked in and strolled to the Juliet balcony to look out at the lights. "It's so beautiful at night."

Jared did the buttons of his shirt up. "One of my favorite cities in the world."

"Which you will never enjoy on your honeymoon because you're never getting married. How sad for you."

"How forward-thinking of me," he retorted. "I can bring my girlfriend here instead of paying for divorce proceedings."

Her throaty laugh did strange things to his stomach. "You think you're so tough, Jared Stone," she murmured as she turned around. "But you're really not. You know that?"

He elected not to respond. She was in white tonight, a simple classy knee-length dress that made the most of her curvaceous figure, hair up in a sleek chignon that left her beautiful neck bare. His strict no-virgin policy should have shielded him from the desire to bury his mouth in the exposed hollow between neck and shoulder. Unfortunately, his body wasn't following his strategic plan.

Biting out a curse, he whipped the tie around his neck and tied it with the quick efficiency of a man who hated that particular accessory. *He was not having her.*

Bailey surveyed him with a critical eye. Walked toward him with a purposeful movement that sent his pulse into overdrive. He yanked in a breath as she came to a halt in front of him and pushed his hands aside.

"Your tie is crooked."

As disheveled as his mind.

He kept his hands by his sides while she undid the tie, set it back around his neck and retied it, her technique smooth and flawless. Her perfume drifted into his nostrils, the curves he was almost going crazy not touching so close he would only have had to take a step to feel her against him.

"How did you," he murmured roughly, "learn to tie a tie so well with no lovers in your life?"

She pursed her lips as she finished it off. "Etiquette training."

"*Etiquette* training?" He stared at her as if he hadn't heard right. "As in Pygmalion?"

She smiled. "If you want to put it like that."

"*Why?*"

Rosy color stained her cheeks. "I grew up dirt-poor with no idea of how to function in society, Jared. I was a stripper. Where was I going to learn what to say over a business dinner? What fork to use? I might have gotten an MBA, but it in no way prepared me for any of that. So I had someone teach me."

"Right." His heart contracted. Just a bit.

Every time he built a wall against her, she disarmed him. She said something like that and reminded him just how vulnerable she was under that tough exterior. It made him want to hold her and never let go.

"Jared—" She bit her lip and stared up at him and God help him, he almost snared that luscious mouth under his and did what he wanted to do. But that was absolutely, definitely not happening. Not tonight when he needed his wits about him. When he needed to *win this deal*.

"We need to go," he announced abruptly, stepping back. "We're already late."

The hurt he seemed to be a professional at putting in her eyes gleamed bright. He ignored it and shoved his wallet into his pocket.

"The car's waiting. Let's go."

The seafood restaurant on the Rue de Rivoli was packed with people on the warm, steamy Paris night. The maître d' led them to the chef's table at the back of the restaurant with its much-in-demand view of the bustling, sparkling kitchen in which white-coated chefs worked in symphonic precision.

They were the last in the group of seven to arrive. Their competition, John Gehrig, the CEO of Gehrig Electronics, rose to introduce himself, his wife, Barbara, and his vice president of marketing. Gehrig was a warm, friendly Midwesterner in his early fifties whom Bailey couldn't help but instantly like. As was Barbara, who was utterly charming as his feminine counterpart, and apparently whip-smart as Gehrig's legal counsel.

She moved to greet Davide, then Alexander, who was superbly dressed in a gray suit and navy shirt and drawing more than one set of female eyes as he stood. He bent to press a kiss to each of her cheeks, the touch of his lips sending an involuntary shiver through her. "You look outrageously beautiful," he murmured in her ear as he brushed the other cheek. "Unfortunate Stone had the pleasure of escorting you."

Bailey stepped back, firmly disengaging his hands. "So lovely to see you again."

Jared made a point of sitting in the seat beside Alexander at the round table designed for conversation, which left Bailey to his left and Barbara beside her. A potent predinner cocktail Barbara suggested was a fine method of relaxation, and before long, the two of them had hit it off.

"So," Barbara murmured as the fish course was being removed, "are you and the delectable Jared together?"

She shook her head. "What made you think that?"

"The way he looks at you. Like he'd like to have you for the main course…you might want to address that."

Or not.

"And then there's the dark and dangerous Alexander…" Barbara mused. "Uncatchable, say the tabloids."

Bailey wondered, for the millionth time, why he was fixated on *her*. Surely the man could have any woman with his looks and fortune?

Jared asked her a question, claiming her attention with a touch of his hand on her arm. It was a gesture that did not escape Alexander's attention because he had been watching her like a hawk all night. Bailey leaned into Jared and contributed her thoughts on the changing retail climate. Alexander tracked the movement. That she heartily enjoyed the constant touching when she was supposed to be hating Jared was a matter she didn't care too examine too closely. It was all an act for Alexander's benefit, of course.

Dinner stretched on, Parisian-style, with course after course of delectable French food. More bottles of twenty-year-old wine were consumed than Bailey could count, accompanied by enough business talk to make the night worthwhile, but not so much it impinged on the very civilized French way of taking the time to truly savor a meal. Talk turned to port when a cheese plate was placed on the table to finish. Davide and Jared, both huge fans of the intensely flavored wine, were invited down to the cellar by the owner to choose their selection. While the Gehrigs went out for a smoke, and their VP left to make a call, Bailey excused herself to use the ladies' room rather than be alone with Alexander.

She took her time, but when she returned to the table, Alexander was still its only occupant. Jerking her head around, she found the Gehrigs chatting to a couple at another table.

Alexander stood. "Sit down, Bailey. I don't bite."

Yes, you do, she wanted to say. But rather than cause a scene, she did. Alexander picked up his wine, lowered himself into his chair, and took a sip. "How did your strategy session go? Ready for Tuesday?"

She nodded. "I think you'll be very happy with the final plan."

"Good." He set the glass down. "Jared may be a maverick but his vision is right."

Her gaze met his warily. "I'm glad you realize that."

His slate-gray eyes glittered. "Why didn't you take me up on that offer in Vegas, Bailey?"

She swallowed. "It wasn't personal. I never fraternized with customers."

"Yet you fraternize with your boss."

Warmth flooded her cheeks. "Jared and I don't have a relationship."

"Oh, come on, Bailey. You're infatuated with him. If you're not sleeping with him now, you will be."

Her blood pressure skyrocketed. "Pick a more appropriate topic or I will leave the table."

"It's fine, you know," he continued. "I only want one night. Think of it like this, my Vegas proposal, except this

time, you don't get fifty thousand dollars, you get to save
your boyfriend's deal."

Her jaw dropped open. "*Why?* Why me, Alexander?
You could have any woman you wanted."

He nodded his head toward Jared's chair. "I want what
he has. I want what I've wanted from the beginning."

She shook her head at the direct, unhesitating stare he
leveled at her. The man was a sociopath.

His gaze narrowed. "For a woman who stripped for
a living you are very naive, Bailey. I want the fantasy. I
want what you were selling on that stage—but I want it
for me. To know when I sink myself into you, I have what
none of them had."

Bailey stood up on shaking legs. "You are insane."

"No," he said underlining the word, "I know what I
want." He nodded his head toward the back of the restaurant. "Sit down. They're coming back."

She turned and saw Jared and Davide winding their
way through the tables, Jared's gaze pinned on her. She
sank back into her chair.

"Don't make a mess of this for Jared," Alexander murmured as the din of the restaurant buzzed on around them.
"Think about it."

She wasn't actually sure what happened the last hour
she sat there in a frozen state. The port was consumed,
the cheese eaten by connoisseurs other than herself, and
somehow the evening ended.

Alexander offered to drive them back to their hotel and
rather than be rude, Jared accepted. When the Frenchman
had dropped them off and they were in the elevator riding
up to their rooms, Jared crossed his arms over his chest,
the hot and bothered look to him suggesting he wasn't so
under control.

"What happened with Alexander at the table?"

She leaned back against the wall of the lift, her head

spinning. "He told me if I took him up on his offer from Vegas, I could save your deal."

His head jerked back. "*What?*"

She swallowed hard. "He said your vision was the future and we were the right choice. But that I could seal the deal by sleeping with him. That he only wanted one night."

His nostrils flared, his fingers flexing around the metal bar that surrounded the lift. She was half terrified he would stop the car and go after Alexander from the coldly furious look on his face. Instead, as the lift stopped at their floor, he stepped out, held the door for her and stalked toward their rooms.

"Your card," he barked, taking it and opening the door. It was a good two or three moments before he spoke.

"What else did he say?"

She lifted a trembling hand to her cheek. "I asked him why. He said he wanted the fantasy. That when he was *deep inside me* he would have what none of the others had." She stared at him. "God, Jared. He's sick."

He was so still, so absolutely still, she could feel her heart pounding in her chest. It throbbed once, twice, three times before he took a deep breath and started toward her, his hands cupping her jaw. "He's a megalomaniac who thinks he can have anything he wants, Bailey. But he will never put his hands on you. I promise you that."

She was shaking. He folded her against his chest and held her there, his hands in her hair. "He's bluffing."

She shook her head. "He brought in Gehrig."

"Gehrig was a natural choice. They're an extremely hot brand. I'm surprised they didn't include them from the beginning. It was a smart move on Alexander's part."

She pushed away. "You need to send me home, Jared. This is crazy."

"Not happening. We have Project X. It's going to win this for us. We stay the course, Bailey."

But he'd never wanted to use his secret launch. They had a whole strategic plan built around the products that involved an array of global partners. And now he was messing with that because of *her* past.

She stalked past him to the closet, pulled her suitcase out and started throwing clothes in.

"What the *hell* are you doing?"

She spun around. "I have to go. It's the only way. If I'm gone, Alexander might lose interest and play fairly."

Hot color stained his cheekbones. "Have you been listening to anything I've said? *He doesn't care*, Bailey. You are not a deciding factor. You are a pawn in his game. So forget anything but us going in there and winning the entire committee over. *Making* him make the right decision."

But what if Alexander didn't do the right thing? She shook her head. "I can't take that chance. I will not lose this deal for you." She turned and started dumping her shoes into the bag, tears stinging the back of her eyes. Jared's hands sank into her waist and spun her around.

"How many times do I have to tell you I'm not doing this alone? We're pitching this together and we're winning."

Her gaze dropped to his perfectly knotted tie. A Windsor knot. Her favorite. And she wondered why, why was he doing this? Why was he backing her to his own detriment?

Her mouth twisted. "He told me he wanted to have what you have. Ironic, isn't it, when you don't even want what I'm offering?"

His gaze darkened to a deep, stormy blue. "You know that isn't true."

"How?" She practically yelled the word at him. "I put myself out there for the first time in my life, we share what we shared and then you shut it down as if I'm totally expendable. A dime a dozen…because of your stupid rules."

His face tightened. "They aren't stupid rules. They're designed to ensure you don't get hurt."

"They're designed to ensure *you* don't get hurt."

He lifted a shoulder. "They are what they are."

"Coward." She hurled the word at him with all the hurt and confusion surging through her. "You talk about trust. You want me to trust you on this, to walk into this pitch with you when you won't even be honest with yourself?"

His cheeks stained deeper. "You want the *truth*, Bailey? You want to know what's been eating at me? I've spent the entire evening, the entire *week* telling myself I can't have you. Telling myself I will hurt you. When all I can think of is *having* you. Teaching you what it's like to be with a man and pleasuring you so much you'll never want another." His blue eyes blazed into hers. *"How messed up is that?"*

Her stomach contracted. Dammit, she wanted that. Jared had *seen* her, the real her, in Nice, and he still wanted her. She'd never felt so stripped down, so vulnerable, so needy of what another person had to offer in her life. And she wasn't questioning it. Not anymore.

"Then do it," she murmured. "Forget about your rules."

"Bailey—"

She silenced him with a finger to his lips. "I don't *want anything* from you, Jared. I don't want promises. I don't want the homestead. But I do want to know what it's like between us. It's burning me up…"

He went so still she wondered if he was still breathing. She stepped into him before he regained the control he always found and cupped his jaw with her palm. "Not one more word. I swear if you say one more word about your rules I'll scream."

Those long lashes settled down over his eyes. Then he opened them and rested his gaze on her. "You sure you can handle this?"

She stood up on tiptoe, balancing her palm against his chest. "You sure you can?"

"No," he muttered. "I am not."

He backed her up against the wardrobe, his suit-clad thigh sliding between hers, his hard gaze full of intent. Thought ceased as he rocked his mouth over hers and took it in a kiss that made her knees go weak. Over and over again, he tasted her, commanded her response until he was the only thing in her head. Until she moved against him and surrendered more of herself. As if he knew exactly what she needed in the way her body softened against his. In the way she accepted his tongue into her mouth and met the erotic slide of it against hers with a low, soft moan that told him she was fully his.

When she was there, fully in step with him, he tangled his hand in her hair, arched her head back and took the kiss deeper, his insistent, bold strokes as he explored her mouth sending a hot, honeyed warmth through her. If he'd lifted his head and told her in that raspy voice of his how he would take her, he couldn't have demonstrated more clearly. She moved against him again, needing more, and this time he dropped his hands down her back, cupped her bottom through the filmy material of her dress and brought her firmly against the hard length of him outlined against the fine material of his pants.

Her half gasp, half sigh reverberated against his lips. His mouth left hers to trail a line of fire across her cheek to her ear. "Be careful what you wish for, sweetheart… you just might get it."

His fingers splayed across her bottom and moved her against him in a delicious slide against the hard, thick length of him, and intimidation faded on a wave of pure, unadulterated lust. She'd heard the other girls in the club going on about their sexual escapades as they'd dressed before a shift, but the way Jared made her feel was…*insane*.

He trailed kisses down the length of her neck to the spot at the base that made her crazy. Made her squirm. Jared lifted his head with a curse, sank his hands into her waist and turned her around so her palms were flat against the wardrobe.

"Enough of that if we're making it anywhere near where we're supposed to."

The rough tone of his voice sent a tremor through her. Being pressed up against the wardrobe made it tunnel deep inside. He lifted her hair away from her neck and resumed his kisses with a slide of his lips against her nape. The soft rasp of her zipper as he multitasked filled the air.

The warm breeze from the French doors slid across her skin as he pushed the dress off her shoulders and let it fall in a swish of fabric to the floor. But it was Jared's hands and lips as they worked their way down her back that had her full attention, making her arch into them and plead for more.

She drew in a breath as he sank to his knees and pressed kisses against the rounded curve of her bottom. His hands were reverent, sure on her skin, as if he wanted to memorize every inch of her. Fire lit her belly, licked at her nerve endings. She was sure she wanted him to. And then he turned her around...

His gaze swept up the length of her, from her legs still clad in high heels, over the curves of her hips and breasts encased in the barest hint of lace, and finally to her face. By the time he got there, she was flushed with self-consciousness and excitement so intense, her breath came in short pulls. Which deteriorated into no breath at all when he slid his fingers underneath the thin strips of silk that held her barely there panties in place and stripped them off.

Her legs went another step toward jelly. If she'd hoped he'd lavish the same attention on her that he had on his knees in Nice, it wasn't to be found as he stood, anchored her against the door and brought his mouth back to hers.

"You are so gorgeous," he murmured against her lips. "My words aren't working."

She melted. Figuratively, of course, because she was still standing when he slid his palm up the inside of her thighs and pushed them apart. Still standing when he cupped the heat of her in his palm in an overt claim of ownership that had her pressing her hands against the wood to keep upright. Her mouth stilled against his, her gasp filling the air as he stroked her. She was hot and wet for him, so turned on she thought she might come apart with the lightest touch. But he claimed her with the slide of his finger instead.

"You'll come with me inside of you this time," he muttered. "And not before."

Bailey tried to keep her head but there was no fighting the mind-numbing pleasure he gave her with the firm strokes of his hand. He urged her thighs wider and slid another finger inside her, stretching her, preparing her. It was so good she could have screamed with the pleasure of it. But he stopped before she could.

"There will be a bed this time." He slid his palm to the small of her back and gave her a gentle push toward it. "Maybe not the next."

She sat on the queen-size bed as he stripped off his clothes and revealed the incredible body she'd seen in swim trunks, but never in tight black boxers that emphasized how very well-endowed he was. Apparently the jokes had been true, she acknowledged with a hellishly dry mouth. Maybe she wasn't so wise to choose him as her first....

If there was any way Jared could have gotten his clothes off faster, he would have. Bailey's unabashedly intent look as he undressed, as if he was putting on a show for her pleasure, did something serious to his insides...left his composure hanging by a thread. And if he'd ever needed composure, now was the time. He'd never taken a virgin. Had no idea what made it a better experience for a woman. Add that to the fact that he'd never wanted anyone as much in his life as he wanted Bailey right now and there were all sorts of ways this could go.

Blocking his mind to anything but her, he moved to the bed and took in how outrageously, spectacularly beautiful she was clad only in a lace bra, curled up with those never-ending legs beneath her. But it was her face that held him. Utterly vulnerable, yet tough at the same time. It was a combination he found irresistible.

He sat down on the bed and pulled her into his lap. Turned her so her knees were on either side of him and they were face-to-face. "I have no idea how some man hasn't persuaded you into bed with him before now, but at this moment, I'm glad of it."

She blinked. "That's quite an admission, Mr. Manifesto."

His lips curved in a wry smile. "I think my rule book's been gone for a while."

He watched her process that. Lifted her hair away from her shoulder and took a mouthful of smooth, silky skin, scoring the surface of the elegant curve with his teeth. He was so hard, so hot for her it took all his willpower to go slow. But that was what she needed and that was what he was going to give her. Even if it killed him.

He slid his lips lower to the swell of her breasts above the lace. She moved her shoulders to help him as he slid the straps of her bra down and stripped it off. His hands moved over the weight of her silky, creamy flesh and cupped her breasts in his palms. She was so perfect, so exquisite, her shaky sigh as he brushed the pads of his thumbs over her rose-tipped nipples almost undid him.

"You ready for me?" he murmured against her mouth. "Because I need to have you *now*."

The way she blindly sought his mouth, wound her fingers in the hair at the nape of his neck, was all the impetus he needed to turn and push her back on the bed. Her gaze was steady, trusting him completely as he ran his palm down her stomach and reclaimed the heat between her thighs.

"I need a condom," he rasped, a last sane thought entering his head. "I'll be right back."

Her delicate fingers grasped his arm. "I've been on the Pill for years for cramps."

That was all the incentive he needed to slide his fingers inside her again, his smooth, rhythmical movements increasing in tempo as he brought her to a feverish, desperate state that would make his possession better for her. When she was twisting, writhing under him and begging for more, he stripped off his boxers and moved between her thighs.

He captured her hands in his and pressed them back against the bed above her head so their fingers were entwined and their eyes locked. "I'm right here," he murmured. "Every step of the way. Guide me."

She nodded. Her gaze clung to his as he brought the hard length of himself against her and teased her with it, back and forth until she closed her eyes and gave a soft moan. "Jared—"

He eased inside her, just the tip to allow her to get used to his possession. She was tight, incredibly tight, and he shook with the control it took to stay there and not move. "Breathe," he instructed huskily. Her chest rose as she did, depressed and rose as she took in another puff of air. And he felt her relax around him. He eased deeper, her flesh clenching him; accepting him and rejecting him all at the same time.

"Bailey—" he demanded roughly, "you okay?"

She nodded. "You feel...amazing."

His soft curse split the air. "Wrap your legs around me, sweetheart. I need more."

She did and he pushed deeper, a fraction at a time, stopping to let her adjust as he went. Finally, he reached the barrier he'd been waiting for, felt her flinch beneath him. He brought his mouth to hers. "I've got to hurt you for just a second and it'll be over."

She nodded and closed her eyes. He claimed her fully, pushing through the barrier with a smooth, sure stroke that made her gasp and twist beneath him. He kissed her through it, holding himself completely, agonizingly still until her body relaxed around his and she sighed into his mouth.

"That's it," he encouraged huskily, "stay with me. You're good now."

He started to move, excruciatingly slowly although his rock-hard body was begging him to go faster. Their hands were still laced together, her eyes glued to his as he caressed her with his pulsing flesh, her muscles clenching him as he withdrew and entered her again and again until she was arching against him and taking him deep.

"You feel so good," he told her, her incredibly tight body fitting him like a glove, making him swell even bigger. "Tell me how you like it. How it feels…"

Her eyes were glazed; she was just this side of incoherent. "So good," she muttered. "So good. God, Jared, don't stop—*please*…"

He released a hand to cup the sexy curve of her hip. To anchor her to him so he could put more power behind his thrusts, hit her in that place that gave a woman the deepest, most powerful orgasm.

"Talk to me," he urged, dangerously close to the edge. "Tell me, Bailey."

"*Amazing*. It feels amazing. Jared—I don't think I can—"

He released her hands and reached between them, setting his thumb against the hard nub of her just above where their bodies were joined. Slowly, deliberately rotated it against her until her hips were writhing against his thumb. She threw her head back and came for him, her body clenching around his so fiercely, it took him only a few strokes to push himself into oblivion. His body exploded inside her, a hoarse cry tearing itself from his lungs as a shattering release swept over him.

It was minutes, long minutes later before his body stopped shaking. Before the chill in the air stole over him. Bailey shivered, her legs still wrapped around him, his flesh buried in hers. And he wondered how he could still be semi-hard after *that*.

He left the warmth of her body to push back the comforter and tuck her beneath it. Bailey protested, a tiny whimper that made him smile. "One second," he murmured, pressing a kiss to her lips. "I am not nearly done with you yet."

He found a bottle of water on the dresser and drank half of it down while he quite frankly tried to compose himself. Because that hadn't been just sex. He felt open, raw, as if someone had stripped off his layers and left him exposed. And the instinct to roll over, to reclaim his power, pulsed through every cell.

Bailey lay there sultry and replete, platinum hair spread across the pillow, gaze tracking him as he drank. Oblivious to the storm in his head. Watching her there, strong, sexy, *unforgettable*, the thought crossed his mind that he could have her a million times and it would never be enough.

His hand tightened around the bottle. *That was truly crazy talk.* No matter how much he'd wanted a woman in the past, it had always faded. Soured. Relationships ended. People got bored. It was just the way it was.

He set the bottle down. Reached for her. Bailey studied his face as he took her in his arms. "You're regretting this?"

He shook his head. *Lied.* "I want more. And I'm not sure you're ready."

She pulled his head down to hers and gave him a long, lingering kiss as her answer. It was all the encouragement he needed to stir to life. He curved his hand around her shoulder, slid it down to press against her shoulder blade and turned her over.

"Jared—" she murmured, a question in her voice.

"I want you this way," he told her softly, pushing her hands apart and moving over her. It was testament to the trust they'd built that she stayed there, her breath picking up in rhythm as he nudged her knees apart, moved between them and pressed openmouthed kisses from the top of her spine to her waist. When she was fully relaxed and supple beneath him, he slid his hand between her legs and stroked her damp flesh.

"Okay?"

"Yes," she moaned, shifting her legs farther apart, pushing up against his touch. It was all the invitation he needed to slide an arm beneath her, lift her and push inside her hot, welcoming flesh with a smooth thrust.

This time he could move slower, build it up, enjoy every centimeter of her undeniably sweet body. When she dug her fingers into the comforter and came with a guttural moan, as if the control he was exerting over her turned her on as much as it turned him on, it destroyed him completely. She was more than a match for him in every way.

He set a palm to the small of her back, held her where he wanted her and chased his own blindingly good release. When it came, tightening his limbs, sweeping through him like the lazy aftershock of a powerful tremor, he knew he'd never experienced such pleasure.

Bailey tucked into his side, curved against his warm body as the filtered Paris moonlight carried them off to sleep, his denial grew weaker. It was useless to pretend even for a second that nothing had changed. Because everything had.

CHAPTER NINE

THE PEAL OF his cell phone in the adjoining room woke Jared at six the next morning. Blinking against the light filtering through the windows, he slid out of bed, grabbed his boxers from the floor and hightailed it into his room in the hopes of catching it before it woke Bailey.

A glance at the call display told him it was Danny, his PI. Kicking the connecting door closed, he took the call.

"Stone."

"You sound half-asleep. Thought you'd be halfway down the Champs-Elysées by now, running your little heart out."

"Eventful night last night." Jared crossed to the French doors and squinted out at the empty Paris streets. "You have something for me or did you just call to pay me back?"

"It's your father. I had my contact do the usual check-in this week. He said he wants to talk to you."

His father wanted to talk to him? He pressed his palm against the elegantly carved mahogany casing of the door. It had been, what, a year and a half, two years, since he'd talked to Graham Stone in a short, curt conversation to sort out some legalities.

"What does he want? Is he okay?"

"He wouldn't say. Says you need to come to him."

His shoulders stiffened. Why should *he* go running when his father had shut him out for almost a decade?

Danny read the pause. "He doesn't look great, Jared. Pretty haggard from what my guy says."

His chest tightened. This was *not* what he needed right now. "I can't go for a couple of weeks."

"I'm just relaying the message. Oh and Jared?" His PI's voice deepened to a satisfied purr. "That dirt you wanted on Michael Craig's proclivity to abuse his expense accounts? I have it. It's bigger and better than you could have imagined."

A twist of satisfaction curled through him. "Send it through. All of it."

He ended the call and tossed his cell phone on the desk. Michael Craig deserved what he had coming to him. What caused an ache to sit low in his chest, ever-present but more pronounced now, was how much he loved his father. Graham Stone had never been too busy, even with his insane hours as a banker, to spend time with his son. Whether it had been building a car or throwing a football around, he'd always been there, even if it wasn't as much as Jared would have liked. Then slowly, in the later years, his father had begun to sink. The massive amounts of stress had finally gotten to him, sending him to a place his youthful son couldn't understand or help him out of.

A fist squeezed his chest, growing larger with every breath. When his father had made his biggest mistake, had stolen that money, it had been too late, far too late to do anything to save his soul. There likely would never be a day on this earth when Jared wouldn't wonder what else he could have done to prevent it. He'd just learned to live with the guilt.

Or had he? The slow burn consuming him didn't make him think so. He'd always thought that walking away, distancing himself from the shame that had enveloped his family, was the right thing to do for his own survival. For his business, where reputation was everything. His father hadn't wanted his help, so what choice had he had?

Light slanted across his face as the sun rose higher in the sky. He had a decision to make. Did he stop running and see what the man who had once been his hero wanted? Or did he wait until it was too late?

Rather than contemplate a question he wasn't prepared to answer, he headed for the shower. It was too late to go back to bed and really, it was the last place he should be. Why he'd thought he could take Bailey to bed in a no-strings arrangement as she'd offered was the joke of the century.

He turned the shower on and stepped under a steaming hot spray. *No strings.* He might as well have handed Bailey the rope and asked her to tie him up in knots. Because if his Zen master had cornered him now and ordered self-awareness, he would have had to admit the only word for last night was…*emotional.* He struggled to get his mouth around the word because it was so foreign to his vocabulary. Emotion didn't figure into his work or relationships. It was an unwise word that made people do stupid things. But he could not deny the truth. He had never felt so connected to another person in his life. And not just because Bailey had been a virgin. It'd been as if he was in her head and she'd been in his.

God. He tipped his head back and sluiced the water out of his face. He'd told himself not to do it. Had warned himself it was a mistake. Why did he continue to let himself want what he couldn't have? How could he be tangling himself up in a woman who was not only the obsession of Alexander Gagnon, she was rapidly becoming *his?*

He tipped shampoo over his head and attempted to scrub some sense back into his brain. He needed to focus on this presentation and win. Take Bailey at her word. It had been one night of ridiculously good sex agreed upon by two consenting adults.

The fact that Bailey had stolen a piece of his heart last night, had been stealing pieces of it for the past week, was inconsequential. He would never be the kind of man who connected on a permanent basis. He didn't have it in him.

It was time he started acting like it.

Bailey leaned back against the bathroom door, nail in her mouth in an absentminded chew as she contemplated an in-the-shower Jared from the perspective of a woman he'd just taken to heaven and back. She was sure no other man would equal his outrageously good body and technique, and had a newfound appreciation for the tennis bracelet club in the Valley.

She replaced the thoroughly chewed nail with another. Last night had been exactly what she'd needed to take her mind off Alexander Gagnon. Except she wasn't sure it'd just been sex. She could have stayed in Jared's arms forever. And *that* was the problem. Not that he'd sneaked out of her bed.

She swallowed hard. Last night had been unforgettable. The heartbreakingly beautiful way Jared taken her virginity, so in tune with her every emotion…how treasured he'd made her feel…how desired.

Oh, Lord. She snaked a hand through her tangled hair. She'd told herself she wasn't getting emotional about this. *Enough.*

She cleared her throat. "Could you tell me where that research is? I want to read it before our meeting."

The click of the shower shutting off should have been her first clue he was getting out. Why she stood there frozen as he shoved the curtain aside and reached for a towel, water dripping off his utterly delicious masculinity, she wasn't sure.

"Sorry, I—" She took a step backward. "I'll wait for you in the bedroom."

"For God's sake, Bailey." He ran the towel over his hair. "You had your legs wrapped around me last night. It's a little late to be embarrassed."

Yes, well, that was last night and this was now. She bit her lip. "Was that your phone I heard earlier?"

He nodded, relieving her immensely by wrapping the towel around his hips. The hard set of his angular face didn't do a great job of reinforcing that comfort, however. His blue gaze was laser-focused and impersonal as he waved his hand toward the bedroom. "It's on the table by the window. Help yourself."

She shifted her weight to the other foot, studied him. *Regret. Definitely regret.* Fine.

"I ordered us coffee and croissants. I'll go read it."

"Thanks."

She waited, a fraction of a second, just to see if he'd have anything to say about last night. Anything that might make today a little less awkward.

The silence was deafening.

She dug her toe into the tile and looked up at him. "It's clear you regret what happened last night."

He gave her an even look. "I don't regret it."

"Then why do you look li—"

"*Bailey.*" His gaze narrowed. "It was great. It was hot. *You* were hot. Absolutely worth it. What else can I say?"

She squinted at him. Had he *actually* just said that?

A sharp pain gouged her insides. "Right," she said, clenching her stomach and pushing past it. "Good to know. And in case you're running a little scared which is wholly possible, you're absolutely right. I meant what I said. It was one night. We're good."

She turned on her heel and left before she became certified dangerous.

* * *

They spent the morning hearing presentations from the marketing and sales groups at Maison headquarters in the Montparnasse district of Paris. Jared thought it interesting that Bailey sat on the other side of the room from him beside an attractive, very young French marketing executive who flirted with her at every possible opportunity. He told himself it was a smart, strategic move on her part, positioning herself as part of the Maison team.

That was before, however, she walked away from him midsentence during a break. Before she blew off his request to get her a coffee.

"Bailey." He kept his voice low as he cornered her on the way back from the machine, coffee in hand. "You know this can't happen between us. It's a bad idea."

She looked up at him, the only sign there was anything going on behind that ice-cold expression of hers the quivering of her bottom lip. "I told you this morning, I *get* it. Hang on to that impressive set of rules, Jared. It's all good."

He stood there, speechless, as she ducked around him and set the coffee down. *Really? She was going to be like that about it?*

The deep freeze continued throughout the afternoon as they toured three of Maison's stores in Paris. Through the cocktails that preceded the French company's annual summer party they'd been invited to attend along with the Gehrig team. He held it together through it all, until they were speaking to the CEO of a Parisian cosmetics company Maison had a partnership with, Jared laying on the charm because the CEO was a great contact to have. Then Bailey rolled her eyes at him. *Rolled her eyes at him* and muttered something about needing to use the ladies' room.

He stared after her, a dangerous heat filling his head. What was wrong with her? *They had the biggest deal of his life to win tomorrow, he had backed her without fail this entire time, and she was acting like a girl over one night together?*

He made it through the rest of his conversation with the CEO, scouted out the washrooms and found them in a hallway off the restaurant. They were one-person affairs, and there were multiples of them. He eyed the one marked women with the door closed, stuck his hand against the wall and waited.

When the door swung open and Bailey stepped out, he pounced.

"Give me a minute, will you?" He bit the words out as he shoved her back into the washroom and shut the door.

"Jared—" She looked up at him with wide eyes. "This is not the place."

"You're *making* it the place." He jammed his hands in his pockets and stared at her. "You told me last night there were no strings. So for God's sake what is *wrong* with you?"

"Nothing." She bit her lip and made a study of the intricate pattern of the floor tiles.

His curse split the air. He slid his fingers under her chin and brought her gaze up to his. The brightness in her eyes made his stomach clench. "Don't you do this to me, Bailey. You promised me you'd be okay with this."

"I am." She pulled out of his grasp and backed up against the vanity. "I guess I'm just not made of stone like you are. Funny," she derided, forcing out a harsh bark of laughter, "women like to use that to refer to a certain body part of yours, but I think it better describes your heart. You can just turn it off and on at will, can't you?"

He looked at her nonplussed. "Apparently not with you, because here I am when I should be schmoozing executives."

"Oh," she choked out. "I think you were doing an excellent job of that."

"Jealous, Bailey?"

She stared him down for a moment, then leaned back against the vanity and ran her hands through her hair. "I just—I don't...I'm just finding it hard to put last night aside. To pretend it wasn't special when to *me*, it was."

He felt his carefully engineered defenses dissolve into dust. Bailey was like a flaw in his perfectly designed ability not to care. A weakness that would surely dismantle him completely if he let it.

"It was...*special* to me too," he admitted, choosing his words carefully. 'I just don't want us to get too carried away here."

"Why?" She poked him in the chest, and *God*, didn't she know by now how much that antagonized him? "What do you think might happen if you let yourself feel? The earth might open up and swallow you whole?"

"No, Bailey..."

"Then *what*? What do you think's going to happen?"

He reached for her then, his hands purposeful as he sank them into her waist and deposited her on the marble counter. "I might do this."

He brought his mouth down on hers in a hot, hungry kiss that was equal parts punishment and absolution. She pushed her hands against his shoulders as if to reject him, but if he was jumping into the fire, then so was she. He cupped her jaw, gentled the kiss and called himself a complete and absolute fool. A sigh racked her as she buried her fingers in his hair and kissed him back, heated and without reserve.

When he finally lifted his head, it was to nudge her thighs apart, step between them and draw her closer. "You are pulling me apart, piece by piece," he admitted huskily. "And I don't like it."

"I don't, either." She reached up and cradled his jaw in

her palms. "But you hurt me this morning, Jared. Be honest with me, yes, but at least explain where it's coming from."

"I'm sorry." He whispered the words against her mouth. Against the velvety softness of her cheek. Against the perfectly shaped earlobe he bit into, sending a shiver through her. It moved through him, made his heart race as his hands went to the hem of her dress and pushed it up, allowing his palms access to the smooth, voluptuous curve of her hip. The scent of her warm, heated flesh filled his head. He slid his hands under her bottom and dragged her to the edge of the vanity. He wouldn't take her here...he just needed to feel her against him.

"Jared—" She moaned his name as if they should stop and start all at the same time. He pulled her hips into his and kissed her. Bailey whimpered and wound her legs around him, and if he'd been inside her it couldn't have felt better than the sweet torture he was inflicting upon himself now.

He lifted his mouth from hers and framed her face with his palms. "As much as I want this, it's not happening here."

She nodded.

He lifted her off the counter and straightened her clothes, then his own.

"I need to fix my lipstick," she murmured, looking a bit shattered. "You go."

He nodded and pulled open the door. Was halfway through it, when he turned back, pulled her into his arms and stole one last kiss. She wound her arms around his neck and kissed him back. He indulged it for a few seconds, then set her away from him.

"We talk when we get back to the hotel, okay?"

"Okay."

He released her and left. He did not see Alexander until

he just about walked into him. Stopping short, his gaze flickered back to the door he'd just exited from.

"Oh, I caught the whole touching kiss." The Frenchman's smile didn't reach his eyes. "Am I allowed to say I'm jealous? Because I am, Stone."

"Why don't we say we're overdue for a drink instead?" Jared resisted the urge to deck him. He was shutting Alexander Gagnon down and he was shutting him down now.

Alexander lifted his shoulders. "If you say so."

Jared led the way to the bar by way of answer, ordered two scotches and took a deep pull of his before he deigned to speak. "Here's how this is going to go, Gagnon. You're going to stay away from Bailey, you're never going to say another sideways word to her, and if you do, I will take you out at the knees."

Alexander smiled, a lazy, loose twist of the lips that wasn't at all concerned. "You have it bad, you know that, Stone?"

He did. He was only beginning to realize how bad.

Alexander eyed him over the top of his glass. "She said you weren't sleeping together."

"Things change." Jared set his drink down, flattened his palms on the bar and leaned forward until the far-too-smooth soon-to-be CEO filled his field of vision. "You aren't ever having her. Get that through your head."

Alexander took a sip of his scotch. "*No* isn't a word I tend to take very seriously. It only makes me want something more."

His mouth twisted. "You couldn't even *buy* her. What makes you think you could ever have her?"

A warning light flickered in those slate-gray eyes, but his shrug was elegantly dismissive. "This deal will make or break you, Stone. Decide your future at a very rocky point in your company's history. Why not set Bailey free for a night? Donate her to the cause? You can put her in the shower afterward and pretend I never happened."

He froze. Clenched his hands by his sides. A fury like he'd never known blanketed him. "You are a sick bastard, you know that?" he gritted out. "She told me you wanted what I have. Well, you will never have what I have, Gagnon. Ever."

Alexander's face tightened. "You are walking a thin, thin line Stone."

"As are you," he bit out, shoving his drink on the bar and pushing to his feet. "I should have taken her under your nose tonight. That would have given me a deep sense of satisfaction."

He walked away before he lost his mind. Then thought he might already have. Because he shouldn't have said that. He should not have gone there.

Bailey reentered the restaurant just as Jared got up from the bar, a coldly furious look on his face, and walked away from Alexander. The matching look the Maison heir wore sent alarm bells ringing through her. What could possibly have happened in the last ten minutes?

Before she could snare Jared and find out, Davide was flagging him down to introduce him to someone. Then they were being rounded up for dinner with both Gagnons, the Gehrig team and several marketing executives from Maison. Jared sat beside her at the round table of ten, quietly seething, leaving Bailey to carry the conversation from their end.

"So," she offered valiantly, "you must all love living in Paris. It's so gorgeous."

Davide nodded. "Although I intend on retiring to the house in the Cap. To me it's *le paradis sur terre*. Heaven on earth."

"Agreed," Bailey nodded. "I love the climate. Perfectly temperate."

"But you must like the extreme heat," Alexander interjected. "Given that you lived in Las Vegas."

The edge to his tone made Bailey set her wineglass down with a jerky movement. "I do," she agreed evenly. "But I much prefer the more moderate Northern California climate."

"Speaking of Vegas," Alexander waved an elegant long-fingered hand at her, "I remembered last night where I met you. I usually have such an impeccable memory…it was driving me crazy."

Bailey froze. Jared's gaze flickered to Alexander, a warning glint in it. "Gagnon—

"It was the Red Room," Alexander continued. "How I could have forgotten when you were so *memorable* I don't know."

John Gehrig's mouth dropped open. The room began to spin.

"Do you know the Red Room?" Alexander turned to one of his marketing executives. The perfectly put together Frenchman shook his head. His boss sat back in his chair and folded his arms over his chest. "You must go the next time you're there. They have the most drop-dead beautiful women on stage; my clients used to salivate. But there was one dancer," he commented, looking over at Bailey, a dark glitter in his silver eyes, "who called herself Kate Delaney who held us all spellbound. We couldn't take our eyes off her."

A buzzing sound filled Bailey's head. Davide gave his son a confused look. "What does this have to do with Bailey?"

"Kate Delaney was Bailey's stage name."

"*Oh*." Davide ran a hand over his jaw and looked at Bailey. "So you were one of those…what do they call them? *Burlesque* dancers?"

"No," Bailey corrected quietly, bile climbing her throat at an alarming rate. "The Red Room is a high-end strip club."

Davide's eyes widened. "A strip club?"

The couple of execs who'd had their heads buried in their smartphones the entire meal looked up, eyes fastening on her. Bailey swallowed hard, heat flooding every inch of her skin. "Yes. It was how I paid my way through school."

A frown creased the elder Frenchman's brow. "That must have been…"

"Lucrative." Bailey dropped her gaze to the candle flickering in the center of the table and absorbed the total and complete silence. Wished she could disappear into the red-hot flame.

John Gehrig cleared his throat. "Well, I for one love the Red Room. The ladies are all just beautiful and I'm sure," he said, shooting a red-faced look at Bailey, "you looked just…lovely."

"There wasn't an unaffected man in the room," Alexander agreed. "Isn't it great to see the American dream alive and well? From stripper to CMO…how *inspiring*."

The bile in her throat threatened to make an immediate appearance. She pressed a hand to her mouth and swallowed hard. Jared made a sound and pressed his palms into the table. Bailey covered his hand with hers. "Don't."

He stared at her hand for a long, hard moment, then lowered himself back into his seat. Davide flicked his son a reprimanding look.

"If you were a gentleman you would pick another line of conversation, Alexander, but since your manners often escape you, *I* will."

Davide started a discussion about foreign exchange rates. John Gehrig hurriedly joined in. Bailey drew in a breath, then another. Told herself walking away from the table right now wasn't an option. But it was painful, physically uncomfortable to sit there with the young executives shooting speculative glances across the table at her. One of them was tapping away on his phone, then slid it discreetly toward his coworker. Photos of her as Kate Delaney no doubt. She'd tried to get the club to sell the promotional photos to her, to take them off the website, and they'd agreed, but nothing ever really disappeared from the internet. It just pretended to.

Jared laid his palm on her thigh. "Breathe."

She pushed his hand away and stared sightlessly out the window at the glittering Eiffel Tower. Felt everything go gray around her as she retreated. She knew the routine. Knew this humiliation like a second skin. It was a familiar, hateful feeling she'd never wanted to feel again.

She drained her wineglass. Smiled tightly at the waiter as he appeared to refill it. Growing up in her house, it had been taboo to say the word *alcoholic*, even though her father had clearly been one and his booze-induced rages had been a monthly fixture. As if none of them said it, it didn't exist.

Apparently she'd also decided to live her life in denial. If she didn't acknowledge the past and the choices she'd made, it could never hurt her. She could go on pretending she was something she wasn't.

But that was all over now. With those men looking at her like this, she felt like a Jenga puzzle someone had pulled the last piece out of.

"I need to go," she muttered in a low, harsh voice to Jared as their dessert plates were cleared. "Tell them I have a headache, tell them I'm exhausted…tell them whatever you want."

She stood up, grabbed her wrap and skirted her way

through the tables to the exit. On the street, she flagged a cab. Jared caught up with her as she was about to slide in.

"Get in," he said grimly, climbing in behind her when she did.

Neither of them spoke until they were in Bailey's hotel suite. She tossed her bag on a chair and turned on him. "Why would he do it? Why would he humiliate me like that? What happened between the two of you?"

Jared sat down on the sofa near the windows. The guilty schoolboy look he wore as he raked his hands through his hair made her heart sink into the ground.

"Alexander saw me coming out of the washroom. He made some comments I couldn't let pass. I figured it was time we had a chat."

She felt the color drain from her face. "We weren't going to do that."

"I changed my mind. I said some things I shouldn't have."

"Like *what?*"

His mouth flattened. "When I made it clear you were with me, he said he didn't care. He said I should take one for the deal. Give you to him for a night then put you in the shower afterward and forget it happened." He pressed his fingers to his temples. "I lost my mind. I went too far."

A wave of nausea flashed over her. "What else did you say?"

"I told him I wished I'd taken you right there under his nose so he would know what he could never have."

Her breath left her. "You didn't."

"I did."

Her hands curled by her sides. "You...."

He stood up. "Bailey—"

"No." She hurled the word at him. "You do not get to be excused for this, Jared. You do not get to be excused for egging him on in some testosterone-fueled duel when

you *knew* what he was capable of. You *knew* he would not hesitate to throw my past in my face."

His face grayed. "I wasn't thinking."

"No—no, you weren't. You were too busy *bragging* about being the one to get me into bed. Making it impossible for him to not retaliate…" She threw her hands up in the air. "My God, Jared, I'm falling for you. *Falling for you*. How could you do this?"

He covered the ground between them with swift steps. The fire in his eyes set her back on her heels. "I have put this deal, this *must-win deal*, on the line for you this entire time, Bailey, because of my feelings for you. So *do not* question my intentions. Yes, I made a mistake tonight…I let my temper get the best of me, and I'm sorry for that. But it's done. And maybe it's a good thing, because you need to move on, you need to stop letting the past hold you captive."

Her eyes widened. "You're kidding, right? You think it's a good thing that the entire table of men I have to present to tomorrow will now be picturing me naked on a stage rather than listening to what I have to say?"

He lifted a brow. "So what? Who cares what they think? You're brilliant. Your ideas are brilliant. You want to defy the naysayers? Prove my manifesto is crap? Then get tougher, Bailey. Get a whole lot tougher than that."

The fists she had clenched by her sides tightened. She thought she might hit him then, and he eyed her as if he would take it. Instead, she felt big, huge, fat tears burning the backs of her eyes and backed away from him before she gave in to them.

"You said earlier you wanted to talk. Let's talk then. This is proving very illuminating."

He shook his head. "I don't think now is the right time."

His eyes said more than his words, the grim look stretching his face making her chest go tight. He was second-guessing what he'd said earlier. Second-guessing his feelings for her after what had happened tonight. After he'd watched an entire table of men react to what she'd been just as he had the first time she'd told him. Shocked. Appalled. She could *see* it on his face.

Anger built inside her, a white-hot storm that was impossible to control. She clenched her hands by her sides. How was it that every man in her life eventually rejected her? Her father, who'd thrown her out? The man she'd liked in Vegas who'd wanted only one thing? Now Jared.

Shame washed over her, stained her skin like a brand. He had treated her like a power play with Alexander because that's what she was to him—expendable.

"Now that you have me," she lashed out, so hurt she couldn't see straight, "why not enjoy the full benefits?" She reached down and yanked her shoe off and threw it at him, a silver missile he plucked out of the air with cat-like reflexes. "I know you're curious," she continued. "You asked me about it in Nice…why not sit back and let me demonstrate?"

His gaze tracked her as she bent her leg and reached for the other shoe. "Bailey—"

Wham. The shoe smacked his outstretched palm and fell to the floor. He took a step forward and reached for her, but she backed away, flashing him a furious look. "*Sit.*"

He sat. Likely because he didn't know what else to do with a crazy woman on the loose. Bailey's fingers moved to the buttons of her shirt, stumbling as she undid them. "That was hot, right, on the sink in the washroom? I'll make it hotter."

He shook his head. "Stop it."

"Oh, come on, you'll love it." She tore at the last button and yanked the shirt off. "Get in the spirit, Jared."

"*Bailey.*" His eyes flashed a warning. "Put your shirt back on."

"Why? All you want is this. You made that clear this morning." She eased her skirt over her hips in a seductive, admittedly angry twist. "All men ever want is this."

He shook his head. "I care about you. You know I do."

She stalked toward him, sank her hands into his shoulders and straddled him. "You wanted to know how I danced for them? How I touched them?" She settled herself into his hard thighs. "Like this…"

He kept his hands stiffly by his sides, anger darkening his face. It made her furious. Made her push her breasts into his chest and rotate her hips against him in a much more intimate caress than she would ever have given a customer. A harsh breath left his lungs.

"You see," she derided, "you can't deny you like it."

"Of course I like it." He clamped his hands around her hips and held her still. "There isn't a second I don't want you. But you are worth more than this."

She shook her head, tears burning the back of her eyes in a glittering prelude to total breakdown. "I saw your face when I told you what I was. You were horrified."

"I was shocked."

"Shocked, horrified…what's the difference?"

He grimaced. "A big one."

She swallowed hard. Dared herself to ask the question that might break her, because how much worse could she feel about herself?

"Could you ever imagine yourself with me, Jared? With all my flaws?"

His jaw hardened. "I've told you I care about you. Stop pushing me."

The warning in his eyes scared her. The sudden, earth-shattering realization that she was undeniably, unmistakably in love with him was worse.

She reached for old habits, old powers as she pressed a kiss to the corner of his mouth. Slid her palm across his thigh to where he lay stiff and thick beneath his trousers. He jerked against her hand and the triumph rocketed through her like a drug she'd been denied too long.

"No."

He dumped her on the sofa so fast it made her head spin. Stepped back. The rebuke in his face made her heart shrivel. "We have a presentation to do tomorrow. We are going in there as a team, Bailey, and we are winning. We are doing what we came here to do. *This,*" he said, glaring at her, "is not happening."

Her lips trembled. "You don't want me."

"You're right," he said harshly. "I want the Bailey I know. The woman who let me look into her soul last night. Not *this.*"

He turned on his heel and left, slamming the connecting door behind him. Bailey curled up in a ball on the sofa and cried. Cried for the girl she'd been. For what she wished she hadn't had to do.

At Jared for being so cruel.

At herself for ruining everything.

CHAPTER TEN

BAILEY WOKE WITH the birds. At some point, after Jared had left, she'd stumbled into bed and slept. Given herself over to a seemingly endless series of dreams whose characters and content overlapped without rhyme or reason, which sent her spiraling into the past, then hurtling forward into the present again in a dizzying journey that ended only with the arrival of the first light of day.

And perhaps the appearance of the loud, squeaky garbage truck that parked outside her window. She winced at the piercing, grinding sound, thinking maybe it wasn't as early as she'd thought, and levered herself into a sitting position. Somehow Paris seemed too elegant a city for garbage trucks…but apparently it too had its baggage it needed to get rid of.

She slid her legs over the side of the bed and padded to the window in time to see the very inelegant green garbage truck move on to the next storefront, hogging most of the narrow street with its robust, squat girth. Watching it made her think. Was Jared right? Was her determination to distance herself from her past destroying her instead of saving her?

She opened the French doors, walked out onto the balcony and braced her palms on the railing. She was proud, extremely proud of what she'd accomplished. Of whom she'd become. If she'd hadn't had the past she'd had, she wouldn't be the person she was now. And maybe that was the way she needed to look at herself: accept the parts she didn't like, the parts she was ashamed of, because they were part of the whole package like it or not.

The cold light of day was telling, exposing, and she shivered against the glare of it. Last night as the world had learned the truth of her, she'd felt as if she'd disintegrated into a million pieces. Funny how you could wake up the next morning and still be here. Could still hurt. Could still be angry.

Could discover that even though you thought the past had the power to destroy you, it really didn't. Not unless you let it.

The graffiti-emblazoned garbage truck turned the corner to meander down the next street, leaving only Jared's stark rejection of her in its wake. She'd spent her life being tougher than all the rest. Refusing to give in when the odds were stacked against her. Which explained why his words had hurt so much last night. She couldn't stand to be a quitter. She couldn't stand for *him* to think she was a quitter.

Couldn't stand for him not to love her.

Her heart squeezed hard in her chest. She hadn't even known she wanted to be loved. Hadn't known she craved it, needed it, like some missing piece of the puzzle that was her until now. It was frightening, *terrifying*, and it had made her drive him away last night—perhaps for good.

She pressed her fingers to the pounding pulse at her temples. Jared wanted a woman *she* didn't even know yet. It was a vulnerable, open version of herself he brought out. Not the old or the new Bailey, something else entirely. It occurred to her that maybe that's who she needed to be. A product of her past but in command of her future.

Increased activity on the street told her it was time to go inside and dress. The pitch was today. And the only thing she *was* certain about this morning was that she had to win this for Jared. Support him as he'd supported her this entire time.

She was dressed in a conservative gray pantsuit when she stopped, high heels in hand. No way was she doing this. Downplaying her femininity just because those men now thought she was entertainment for hire.

That would be letting them win.

She shrugged out of the suit and reached for the new chic mauve one she'd purchased on a whim on the Champs-Elysées. The material was gorgeous and the skirt showed a lot of leg.

Jared knocked on the door just as she'd finished dressing. His mouth curved as he looked her over. "That your battle gear?"

"Something like that."

He stepped closer and tucked a chunk of her hair behind her ear. "There isn't another person I'd want by my side today."

The dark glimmer of emotion in his eyes sent a flicker of hope through her. "Nor I."

She led the way out of the room. Today wasn't about emotion. Today was about getting the job done.

Jared spent the short ride from their hotel to the Maison offices finding his center. He'd spent the night sleepless and keyed up, not just because of what had happened with Bailey, but because this was it. One way or another his future would be determined today. He was done romancing the board, done proving himself when that's all he'd done over the past ten years to make money for his shareholders. They had to climb aboard his vision, understand where the future was, or he was out.

He stared out the window, watching the mad drivers dart in and out of traffic with an early-morning fervor that was just this side of frightening. Winning the Maison partnership would be an incredible achievement. He could transform the consumer electronics industry with it. But he could no longer sacrifice his soul for the company he'd built. Maybe it was the summons from his father that had done it, the knowledge that life was finite. But he knew the path and it wasn't this.

He didn't need a trek to the Himalayas to find peace. He needed to trust himself. And he wanted to be back in his labs creating with the engineers.

The car rolled to a halt in front of the skyscraper containing the Maison offices. The Gehrig team had already pitched when they walked into the metal-and-chrome boardroom, filled to the brim with the marketing, PR and sales teams. He read the atmosphere: alive but not buzzing. And knew they just had to set the room on fire and the deal was theirs.

If Alexander Gagnon played fairly. Gagnon was uncharacteristically subdued as he introduced them to the heads of the key departments. They socialized for a few minutes, then began. Adrenaline surged through him as he walked to the front of the room and opened with the history of Stone Industries, the "why us" argument and the successful alliances his company had forged around the world.

By the time he'd laid the groundwork, given an impassioned speech about vision, the room was noticeably energized. He handed the clicker over to Bailey, who looked calm and composed. Gobsmackingly stunning. "We've got this," he murmured. "Bring it home."

She nodded and walked to the front of the room. There wasn't a male eye that wasn't on her behind in the beautifully tailored suit as she stopped and turned around. He was pretty sure the hushed whispers had more to do with the gossip from last night than the subject at hand, and apparently Bailey had figured that out too, a shadow falling across her face. He watched her blink, then visibly check herself. Pull her shoulders back. And begin.

She launched into her slides with an easy, firm command of her ideas. Laid them down as if everyone in the room better be in the game or they were missing something special. Head thrown back, she roamed the room, keeping their interest, soliciting their response. And when the arrogant young marketer who'd passed her photo around last night started a side conversation with a coworker that clearly had nothing to do with the presentation and everything to do with Bailey's assets, she stopped by his chair and asked him if he had a question. Davide's mouth twitched, the marketer shut his and sank back into his chair, and Bailey moved on.

Jared leaned back and simply watched. He didn't sit poised to jump in and help her. Wasn't concerned a fact might be wrong. He knew Bailey now, knew he could trust her. What he was fascinated with, however, was *this* Bailey. He'd seen her confident before, seen her unsure in her own shoes and overcompensating. But he had never seen this version. *Commanding. Fierce. Combative.* And he knew in that moment he'd been wrong the day they'd driven in from the airport into Paris. Bailey was *more* than any man had a right to expect in a woman. She was courageous and vulnerable and stunningly brilliant, everything he'd been convinced didn't exist in a female.

She made him feel things he'd thought he'd never experience for another human being. Realize he was capable of it. And knew she'd been right; he was afraid. Afraid of making the same mistakes his father had made. Afraid of loving a woman who might leave.

Afraid of facing the truth of himself.

He shifted in the chair, his clarity unsettling. Bailey had never had love in her life, never had someone to protect her. Yet she was courageous enough to open herself up in the hopes she might someday have it. He was pretty sure he wanted to be that for her. To be the one to protect her. To believe in her.

He was scared he wanted all of her. Frightened it wasn't within his realm.

He raked a hand through his hair, his guts doing a fine job of rearranging themselves as Bailey sat down beside him, a rosy glow in her cheeks.

He gave her a sideways look. "Where did *that* come from?"

"Garbage trucks."

"Garbage trucks?"

Her mouth curved. "I'll tell you later."

Alexander opened the room to Q&A. There was a spirited debate about their direct-to-consumer ideas, their unorthodox retail strategy. But a seemingly general agreement the ideas were inspired. Alexander spoke last, directing a hard look at Jared. "All very impressive, Stone. We'd no doubt make a great partnership together. But when it comes down to it, it's the products that will win, not the marketing. And to me, you and Gehrig are neck and neck."

Fair point, Jared conceded. If you looked at the here and now. He stood up and walked to the front of the room to advance the slides.

"I'd like," he said, pausing for emphasis, "to introduce you to Project X."

The room buzzed as he unveiled his next generation product line: phones, tablets, computers, home alarms, thermostats all linked by a common platform—the connected home realized. No company, anywhere, had anything like it, and he felt the energy of the room skyrocket as the questions came fast and furious. *How quickly can you bring it to market? Would people really pay that much for a thermostat that controlled their house? Can it really do that?*

Alexander watched it all, a smile playing about his lips. As if he knew Jared had won. As if he wasn't sure he had a choice anymore.

He said nothing until it was just them and Davide in the room. "You didn't deign to enlighten us about Project X before now?"

"No," Jared said deliberately, "I didn't."

Alexander's eyes glittered. "I'll give you a decision within the week, then."

Jared nodded. Said his goodbyes to Davide. The older Frenchman looked heartsick as he kissed Bailey goodbye, and Jared had to smile. She had that effect on men. Now what was he going to do about it?

CHAPTER ELEVEN

FOR THE FIRST hour and a half of their flight back to San Francisco, Jared tore through the wrap-up from their presentation with quick efficiency. He fired a list of to-dos at Bailey, marked items for follow-up and outlined his vision for how he saw their marketing evolving. He wanted to expand her ideas to other partners, make them a cornerstone of their strategy, and although she loved the idea, she was too tired, too emotionally exhausted and too wary of him to really take any of it in.

Were they ever going to have that talk or was he just planning on forgetting they had ever happened?

Her stomach rolled. Had she turned him off that badly?

Jared repeated something in that relentless, authoritative tone that was getting on her nerves.

"What?"

He gave her a long look. "Need a break?"

She threw her notebook on the table in answer, stood and crossed to the tiny windows to stare out at the inky darkness. The snap of his laptop closing cut across the silence.

"Consider our business concluded for the evening, then."

Something, some edge to his voice made her turn around. He was watching her with that strange, contemplative look he'd been giving her all day since they'd walked out of the Maison building, their presentation behind them.

He pressed a button on the console and asked the attendant to serve the champagne.

She lifted a brow. "We haven't won yet."

"You need to be a more positive thinker."

Her chest tightened, lifting her shoulders. "Alexander could still follow through on his threats, Jared. Choose Gehrig."

"He won't. He wants Project X."

"And if he continues to play games for the sake of it?"

He lifted a shoulder. "Then I'll reinvent myself. Frankly, I'm very much in the mood."

He was in *some* kind of mood, that was for sure. Another side of him she couldn't read.

Betty, a young, attractive twenty-something brunette with an eye for Jared, bustled in with the champagne and poured it into two flutes.

"Get some rest," Jared told her. "We won't be needing you anymore."

The brunette put the champagne bottle in the ice bucket, flashed Bailey an "I am so jealous" look and disappeared.

Jared picked up the glasses and crossed over to hand one to her. Warmth seeped into her cheeks as his fingers brushed hers. "You know what she was thinking."

His blue eyes glittered with intent. "Then she'd be right wouldn't she? I don't intend to spend the next thirteen hours studying our stock price."

Her pulse sped into overdrive. "We haven't even talked yet."

"So let's talk." He lifted his glass and tipped it at her. "You were magnificent in that room today, Bailey. Absolutely brilliant. You have earned my trust, earned my respect. You can stand by my side any time and I would be lucky to have you there."

Oh. She rocked back on her heels. His gaze remained on her, purposeful, intent. "You had the room in the palm of your hand. Including me."

Her stomach contracted. "I don't know about that." She rested her glass against her chin, "The garbage trucks woke me up this morning. And there I was standing at the window watching them and I knew you were right. If I don't deal with *my* garbage, with my past, and accept that it's a part of me, I will never truly move forward." She looked up at the man who had never doubted her, not even once, when so many people in her life had. "I wanted to win this for you. That's all I knew."

He captured her free hand in his and tugged her forward. "I didn't walk away from you last night because I didn't want you, Bailey. I walked away because I wanted *that* woman, the woman who blew my mind in that boardroom today."

She pulled her bottom lip between her teeth. "I'm still figuring out who she is."

"I know," he said softly. "Every time I watch you struggle and triumph, it touches something inside of me. I can no more remain immune to you than I can stop the sun from rising in the morning. And that terrifies me."

Her heart slammed against her chest, loud and insistent.

"Last night," he admitted, tracing his thumb over her cheek, "the thought of Alexander getting anywhere near you made me crazy. I had to tell him he would never have you because *I* want you. I don't want anyone else to have you. But I've never been *that* man, Bailey, the man who sticks. I don't even know if I'm capable of it."

She pulled in a breath, but the air in the tiny plane suddenly seemed nonexistent. The joy exploding inside her that she hadn't ruined everything was almost overwhelming. "Maybe we both need to try…" she managed to get out. "Try to move beyond our pasts."

His mouth twisted. "We're quite a pair, no?" He hooked his fingers in the waistband of her skirt and pulled her flush against him.

Her lashes drifted down as heat ignited inside her. "We make a good one, though."

He nodded, his gaze resting on hers. "You said you'd settle for a man who respects you. A man who tells the truth. A man who wants you for who you are. I cannot, will not, make promises I'm not sure I can keep. But I can promise you those things, Bailey. And I'm willing to try with the rest."

Emotion clogged her throat, so big, so huge, she felt as if she might choke on it. She didn't need his promises. It had never been about that with them. It had been about trust. And for the first time in her life, she trusted a man explicitly, without reservation.

"Last night might not have been the last time you need to pick me up," she murmured, offering him an out. "I am definitely a work in progress."

He brought his mouth down to brush against hers. "Consider me on board."

He kissed her then, a long, lingering promise of a kiss that lit her from the inside out. Her arms crept around his neck. He ditched their glasses, swung her up in his arms and carried her into the bedroom at the back of the plane. It was tiny, dominated by a king-size bed and a chest of drawers, and when he set her down on the soft carpet and sat on the bed, her pulse rate skyrocketed.

"Last night," he murmured, leaning back on his palms, "I didn't want sex between us to be about anger. I didn't want you lowering yourself to that. But tonight," he amended huskily, his gaze on hers, "feel free to demonstrate."

She stared at him. "Jared—"

He shook his head. "I don't want that memory between

us. The thought of you doing this for me is a massive turn-on, Bailey. For no other reason than you are you and you do that to me. Not because you did it for hundreds of other men who couldn't have you and I can."

The heat in his gaze got her. The deep, powerful throb of the jet beneath her feet mirrored the one pulsing between them. Her head went there and then her body followed. She *wanted* to do this for him. She wanted to wipe away the memory of last night.

She bent her leg and tugged a shoe off. He held up his hands, eyes glittering. "No missiles, please."

She tossed the shoe on the floor. Reached for the second. Then she moved forward to stand in front of him. His electric-blue eyes darkened into deep metallic as she reached for the top button of her blouse.

"There are rules," she murmured. "No kissing and no touching."

His gaze narrowed. "I think I've changed my mind."

"No, you haven't." She took her time, working her way down the buttons. Watched him as she stripped off the shirt and dropped it to the floor. His gaze fell to her breasts encased in cream-colored lace, her nipples already hard and pressing insistently against the confining material. He swallowed hard.

"Still want to change your mind?"

"No," he rasped. "I'm good."

She straddled him. Waited for the detached feeling that always came with this. But his eyes wouldn't let her; they held hers firm and forced her to connect. With Jared there was only the truth. There only ever had been.

His heavy-lidded stare dropped to her erect, pink-tipped nipples. "I'm not sure why they call this a lap dance. Feels more like torture to me."

"Yes," she agreed, "it could be described that way. Except," she murmured, rotating her hips in a seductive circle against him, "if you're a very good boy you might get more."

He muttered something under his breath she thought she deciphered as, "I sure hope so," and closed his eyes.

He was hard beneath her, thick and long under his suit pants, and this time it was she who swallowed. She remembered how he had filled her. Remembered how her muscles had clenched around him and how powerful her release had been. *Lord.*

She kept up her sinuous rotations. His thighs tensed beneath her, his hands fisting at his sides. "This better be special treatment, Bailey. Because if you did this for another man, I might have to kill him. Kill them all."

She leaned down and gave him a kiss. "Easy, tiger. It is."

He slid his hands over her hips. She removed them. "No hands."

"But you just kissed me…"

"That's because I'm in charge."

Ruddy color dusted his cheekbones. "Go ahead, convince yourself of that."

"No hands," she repeated, swaying closer. "Lips, however, are allowed."

He dipped his head and took her engorged nipple in his mouth. The hot warmth of his lips around her sent a bolt of heat to her core. She arched her back on a low moan and gave herself to him, wholly, sinfully, rocking against him.

He transferred his attention to the other hard peak and took her higher. She felt herself unraveling under his touch, losing the control she'd once so desperately craved. But this was Jared, and she was mad about him.

"Goddammit, Bailey." He lifted his head, eyes glittering. "I'm waving the white flag, whatever you need."

She stood up and slid her skirt off. Her panties. His gaze tracked her every movement, hot, hungry. She came back to him, moved her fingers to the button of his trousers and slid it out of the material. Then she eased his zipper down.

"Please," he was begging now. "Hands are good. I do good things with them."

She freed him from his boxers. Lowered herself to brush against the hard, hot length of him. "No hands."

She was slick and fully aroused, but he was a lot to handle. It took all her concentration to take him inside her, ease herself down on the potent length of him. She hadn't taken half of him when a low groan escaped her lips. "Jared—"

"Oh yes you can," he rasped, reading the look. "But you need to let me use my hands."

She nodded. Closed her eyes as his palms took the weight of her hips and held her over him, sliding farther inside her. He held her there while her body adjusted to him, his superior strength sending a surge of lust through her.

"More," she groaned.

He gave it to her, slowly, inch by inch, whispering in her ear how much he wanted her, how good she felt. His sexy voice excited her, inflamed her, softening her body until she took him all. It was all she could do to breathe with him buried inside her, but his hands supported her hips, controlling the rhythm, easing her into it.

The feeling of intense fullness morphed into a slow, hot burn every time he took her. The angle, the spot he was reaching deep inside her, promised extreme pleasure. Higher and higher he led her until it wasn't enough anymore—until she wanted to scream. She buried her hands in his hair and pleaded in a husky tone she didn't recognize as her own.

He slid his hand between them and pressed his thumb against the throbbing center of her. She looked down, watched him, the erotic sight of the rough passes of his thumb over her throbbing center summoning a wild, shattering release within seconds, her love for him escaping her lips as the white-hot intensity tore her apart.

He heard her, she knew, from the way he froze beneath her. Then the tight convulsions of her body around him pushed him over the edge, an animalistic groan tearing itself from his throat. And then there was no room for thought. Only pleasure.

The fact that he didn't repeat her words as he settled her against his chest and put his lips to her hair, his breathing hard and uneven, didn't completely throw her. This was Jared, after all, who'd just taken a huge step in telling her how he felt. She was going to focus on that and nothing else. Not on the very real possibility he would never get there.

She woke by the light of the moon, by herself in the bed. A glance at the clock told her it was almost eleven, another couple of hours before they would land. She sat up, looking for water, figuring Jared had left her to work. As her eyes adjusted to the darkness, she saw him sitting in a chair by the windows, dressed only in jeans. He looked lost, distant, in his own world.

"Couldn't sleep?"

He lifted his head. Blinked. "No." He didn't invite her over but she went anyway, setting her hand on his shoulder. His stiffness beneath her fingers made her hand still. The utter remoteness on his face made her consider retreating, until he reached up and pulled her down on his lap. Her heart squeezed at the near rejection. He was such a complex, multifaceted man. She was sure she only knew pieces of him.

She stayed there, curled against his chest, until the restlessness emanating from him made her draw back. She traced the hard line of his jaw, the unyielding curve of his mouth, the jagged white scar that bisected his upper lip. "How did you get this?"

He frowned, as if he had to pull the memory from the deep recesses of his mind. "The son of one of our friends my father embezzled the money from went to Stanford with me. After my father was sent to jail, he confronted me in one of the campus bars. He was angry, said some things about my father I couldn't let pass, and we got into a fight." His mouth twisted. "I thought it was a fistfight, but when Taylor started to lose, he added a beer bottle to the mix."

She shivered as she looked at the vicious-looking inch-long scar. "He could have done much worse."

His shoulder lifted. "He was hurting. His family was ruined. I got it."

She ran her fingers across the heavy dark stubble on his cheek. "You were too. Couldn't he see that you weren't to blame for your father's actions?"

"When you're angry and sad, you lash out."

Yes, but it hadn't been his burden to carry. Her heart squeezed. How hard must it have been for a college-aged boy to have to defend his hero.

He pulled her tight against his chest, his hand smoothing her hair. "My father wants to see me. That call you heard yesterday morning was my PI saying he'd done his usual check on him, that he didn't look great and he wants to see me."

The call that had come right before he'd gone ice-cold on her…it made sense now.

"Do you know why?"

"No."

"Are you going to go?"

"I don't know. When he got out of jail, he told me he needed time to get his head together, to figure out what he wanted to do. My mom had already remarried, and many of his friends wanted nothing to do with him. I was it really for him, but he didn't even want to see me. He disappeared, showed up in the islands. I told myself distancing myself from him was the best thing for me. I was hurting so badly, *I* needed space. But we never really reconnected after that, except over legalities. Every time I tried, he pushed me away."

"I'm sure he felt a lot of shame."

His fingers traced the curve of her ear. "I think I was afraid to face what had become of him. He was such a strong, proud man. Afterward…it was like seeing a ghost of him."

Her heart contracted in another long pull. She took his hand in hers and laced her fingers through his. "That could never happen to you. You are self-possessed in a way I have rarely seen, Jared. You know who you are."

His fingers tensed beneath hers as if he might pull them away, then he let out a breath and curled them tightly around hers. "I should have gone to see him. I should have insisted on it instead of just having him watched over. He's my father, for God's sake. He's not well and I've let him become a virtual hermit."

She shook her head. "You were hardly more than a boy when he left. You were sad and angry because he was supposed to take care of you."

"It doesn't excuse my behavior."

"It's never too late to make it right."

There was a long pause. Her fingers tightened around his. "Go, Jared. Talk to him. You won't forgive yourself if you don't."

He was silent then. She curled into his chest and tried to absorb his tension. But this part of Jared, this haunted part, was one only he could deliver himself from. Forgive himself for. She felt it rise up between them like a physical presence as the minutes wore on, creating a distance she couldn't bridge.

She got the message. Dressed and went back into the cabin and asked Betty for a cup of tea. Then sat watching the night as it sped by. Did people ever truly slay their demons? Or was it just easier to accept them as a part of you? She had always done that, but Jared had convinced her to try harder. Now if he could only do that for himself.

CHAPTER TWELVE

THEY NEEDED GLAMMING up.

Bailey came to that decisive conclusion about her slides for the executive committee meeting about the same time she remembered that the steaming Americano her colleague had brought her as reinforcement was sitting untouched on her desk. Tugging the top off the coffee, she brought the steaming brew to her lips. Maybe she needed some graphs. Clip art? Or maybe a joke…those meetings always needed livening up, didn't they?

And where had her concentration gone? She'd been doing so well all morning, ignoring the fact that Jared returned from the Caribbean today. Ignoring the fact that she was dying to see him to the point she really had to wonder about herself. She wanted to know how things had gone with his father. She wanted to know if he'd heard from Alexander. *And shouldn't he be in by now?*

A smile curved her lips. She hadn't needed to convince herself things could be different since she'd returned from France a week ago. They *were* different. She was the CMO of this vibrant, innovative company, she had a gazillion ideas in her head she couldn't wait to execute and yes, there was that little detail that she was in love with her boss.

A zing of anticipation ratcheted through her, sparking a warm glow in her cheeks. She'd spent two nights at Jared's place before he'd left. Two perfect nights in his stunning Pacific Heights mansion cooking together, getting to know each other and finishing off whatever work they'd had. And yes, countless hours in Jared's bed learning each other in different ways. It had been so good, so intimate, she'd laughingly threatened to bake the next time she'd come over. Except the next time hadn't come until the night before Jared had left to visit his father, and he'd been so keyed up about it, it had been a certified disaster.

In the days leading up to the trip, she'd watched him grow increasingly agitated. About everything, she suspected: the board meeting, the deal, the trip. She'd offered to cook for him that night thinking maybe she could distract him. Tempt him with a passionate night in bed. But he hadn't been there, not really. He'd toyed with his dinner, a distant look on his face, and cut the night short after they'd finished, pleading an early flight.

She'd tried not to remember his sarcastic line in Nice about kicking a woman out after they'd cooked for him, but that's exactly what had happened. And she, who wasn't at all sure what being in a relationship entailed, hadn't really known how to analyze it.

Was he pulling back? Did she just need to give him space because of his father? Was she supposed to be unnerved he hadn't returned any of her texts while he was away except to say that, yes, he'd landed fine?

Her heart thumped nervously in her chest. She supposed she was about to find out when he did come in. Which was a good thing because she needed to ground herself. Being with Jared had made it clear her job wasn't enough anymore. That being with someone as she was with him was something she'd been missing her entire adulthood. She *did* want the house and the white picket fence, as long as he was in it. As long as they were equals. And although she knew she needed to take it step-by-step with him, although the idea terrified her as much as it did him, she wanted to know she could have it. That this was real.

The slides stared back at her—clearly lacking. She needed to have them done for Jared so he could review them before they presented at tomorrow's board meeting. With a sigh, she put her coffee down and went searching for clip art.

Tate Davidson waltzed by her desk, leaving a trail of his sleazy cologne. "Big guy's in fine form."

Her gaze whipped to him. "Jared's back?"

"Sure is." He lifted a brow. "Surely he's checked in with his *CMO*?"

She lowered her head and ignored the dig. Tate was insanely jealous she'd been promoted over his head. And more importantly, her brain whirred, Jared was back. How long had he been in? Why hadn't he come to see her?

Her phone rang. She barked a greeting into it. It was Nancy from HR, wanting to schedule a meeting. "Sorry, what is this for?"

"Your sixty-day check-in."

She frowned. "What sixty-day check-in?"

"The one that's in your contract," Nancy said patiently. "Jared wanted to review things at the sixty-day mark."

He did? Wasn't it usually ninety days? Having signed the contract and not read it thoroughly before they'd left for France, she wouldn't know. She whipped it out of her drawer and scanned it. There it was on page eight in the fine detail. *Employee Trial Period*: *Employee's performance in the role to be reviewed at the sixty-day mark.*

"Isn't it usually ninety days?" she asked Nancy.

"Often, yes, but this is a high-profile role. Jared wanted to make sure he wasn't making any mistakes."

Mistakes? Her blood flashed hot in her veins as she kept reading, scanning through the legalese. *This position can be terminated for any reason determined by the employer, not limited by underperformance.*

"And *this* termination clause…*can be terminated for any reason?* Is this normal?"

There was a pause. "That's a little more…stringent than usual. But again, a high-profile position."

Bailey stared at the words. That clause said Jared could demote her for any reason after two months regardless of her performance on the job. Any clause she'd ever had in a contract had been based on performance.

She pulled in a breath. "You know what, Nancy? I'm going to schedule this check-in myself. Consider it done."

"Yes, but Bailey we don't do it that wa—"

Slam. She whacked the earpiece on the base. Shot to her feet. The hallways flashed by in a stream of silver as she made her way to the elevator and up to the executive floor. Mary, Jared's PA, gave her a bemused look as she stormed past her, knocked once on his door and flung it open.

Jared was bent over a pile of papers, a frown on his face. He looked up in surprise, flicked his gaze over her and rose to close the door.

"What's wrong?"

"First of all," she bit out, "it's nice that Tate Davidson knows you're back. It would also have been nice to get an answer to one of my texts. I know you're a very busy, important man but I would have enjoyed that courtesy."

His face softened, and now she could see the lines of fatigue crisscrossing it. "I'm sorry. I was on my way down after lunch."

"Two." She waved the contract at him. "Did you instruct HR to put that clause in my contract? The one that allows you to demote me *for any reason*, regardless of my performance?"

His frown deepened. "Yes. But that was before I knew what you were capable of."

She crinkled up her face. "You stood here and agreed to my terms. You asked me to come to France, to *save* your reputation and win that contract, when you weren't intending on *honoring* our deal?"

He walked toward her, his hands raised as if she were a child who needed to be calmed. "You were an unknown quantity, Bailey. I could hardly make you CMO without an opt-out. Be reasonable."

"An opt-out?" Her voice lifted a notch. "That clause is way beyond an opt-out. It's an ironclad opportunity to get rid of me whenever you so choose. Even Nancy said it was unusually…what did she say? Oh, *stringent*, that was the word."

"Bailey," he said quietly, holding her gaze, "that clause has nothing to do with the here and now. You have proven yourself to me. The job is yours. If you like, I'll have another contract drawn up."

"What I'd *like* is to know that you believed in me from the beginning. That you are a man of your word and you were going to honor our agreement."

He blanched. "Trust is earned."

"And I gave it to you *every step of the way*." She flung the words at him as she brought herself within inches of his tall, imposing figure. "I opened myself up completely to you, Jared. I let you break me down. And all I required in return was the honesty you promised me."

He shook his head, eyes flashing. "Everything I said to you, promised you over the past couple of weeks, is true, Bailey. Do not let *this*, do not let your insecurities, ruin a good thing."

"A good thing." She barked the words out, hands on her hips. "How long should I expect this *good thing* to last, Jared? A couple months? Three? Four? You were already backing off the other night as per usual. Then you go completely incommunicado."

He shook his head. "I've been up to my ears, stressed about my father..."

"So you shut me out?" She pressed her lips together, the insecurity, the hurt she'd felt over the past few days, sitting like the devil on her shoulder. "I'm no expert but I'm pretty sure this is where we're supposed to lean on each other. Be there for each other."

His mouth tightened. "I've been trying. You push too much, Bailey."

The stubborn tilt of his chin, the forbidding line of his mouth, did her in. "I know you heard me say I love you on the plane, Jared. You ignored it completely."

He shook his head, his face losing color. "I told you I don't make promises I can't keep. It isn't in my DNA. You knew that."

He could have said anything, *anything* but that and she might have been okay with it. But a cop-out like that? It made her chest feel so tight she couldn't breathe. Because it wasn't enough anymore. Not when she'd handed him her heart.

She nodded sagely. "Now there's the honesty I need. Because I've decided I can't do this, Jared. You asked me to open up, to trust you. Well here I am. And if you can't do the same, I think we should end it now."

His gaze flashed. "You're using this as an excuse to end things before it's started."

She shook her head. "This is me not wanting to be another casualty of the cult of Jared. I guess it's not in *my* DNA to expect anything less than everything."

"Bailey—" He reached for her, but she shook him off, stalked to the door and left. Enough of this emotional roller coaster.

Jared was debating whether to go after Bailey when Mary stuck her head in his office. "Alexander Gagnon is on the line."

He cursed. If there was a person he did not want to talk to at this moment in time, it was Alexander. However, as the fate of his company lay in the man's hands, he had no choice but to.

He shut the door, walked to his desk, sat down and took a deep breath. Then he hit the blinking line.

"Gagnon."

"*Bonjour,* Stone." Alexander's smooth, silky voice slid over the phone line. "Good news for you. We have decided we would like to offer Stone Industries the partnership."

The rush of satisfaction that ran through him at Gagnon's words was swift and sharp. But the burn that stung his eyes, the tremor in his hands as he pressed them against his desk, came from a deeper place. A place he'd been loath to acknowledge. He would have walked, he'd been prepared to walk, but *this* was his company. To restore what he'd built with his heart and soul to its former brilliance— he wanted it with every fiber of his being.

"Thank you," he rasped. "I'm very happy to hear that."

"This is dependent, of course," Gagnon said, "on Project X being exclusive to our stores."

"Certain product lines, yes, but not all."

"We can come to some kind of an agreement on that, *oui*. We will need to work very closely together in the beginning. The planning will be key. I want Bailey in Paris for quarterly meetings. How is your beautiful CMO, by the way?"

Jared sat up straight. "Bailey is not part of this deal, Gagnon."

"So vehement," the Frenchman chided. "I merely want her brain. What are you going to do, Stone? Marry her? That would certainly keep the dinner conversation interesting."

His blood bubbled dangerously close to the surface. He

thought he might, actually. Want to marry her. Watching her walk out of his life could do that.

He stared viciously at the phone. "Send the contract over, Gagnon. And forget about Bailey in Paris. You'll have Tate Davidson, my VP."

He ended the call before he said something to trash the deal. Sat back and tried to digest. He was overwhelmingly relieved to be walking into that board meeting tomorrow with Maison in his pocket. Michael Craig's massive abuse of his expenses as CEO had been splashed across the news this morning in a carefully executed plan to discredit him and oust him from the Stone Industries board, thanks to a friendship Jared had with a high-placed reporter at a daily newspaper. Everything was falling into place. But it was Bailey who occupied his head. He'd had to put that clause in her contract. He was running a multibillion-dollar company. He didn't put someone whose ability he'd questioned into a C-suite position without a backup plan.

His chin jutted out, his resolve fierce. Except she was right. He'd promised her the job. The clause should have been about performance. Instead he'd been intent on manipulating the situation to his advantage. That was the real truth. He'd been running as fast as his legs could carry him the last few days.

Bailey was right.

His time in the Caribbean had been mind-altering. Just as terrifying as he'd anticipated. His father was a shadow of his former self; old, suffering from debilitating diabetes and wanting his son to know the truth after reading his manifesto. It had not just been his marriage that had brought him to his knees, his father had told him, but his lack of faith in himself. His inability to follow his dreams. But Jared, he'd counseled, a wisdom in his eyes that seemed out of place in such a weak, frail man, had done just that. He had followed his heart, and that's all a man could do.

You cannot, his father had warned him, *take on my legacy, or you will destroy yourself.*

Achingly honest, frighteningly intense, his conversations with his father had nearly undone him. Had left him shaken and angrier than ever at himself. He should have done more. He should have done something sooner. *He* should have been braver.

The burn in his eyes brought a hot glitter to his vision. He was not his father. He knew that. And Bailey wasn't his mother. He had spent the flight home thinking about the two of them, how very different they were. His mother was brittle, power-hungry, content to live life on the coattails of each successive powerful man she conquered, whereas Bailey was strong in a beautiful, courageous way. Independence personified. You could see how much she cared in her eyes just now. Funnily enough, what he'd thought would never work for him was now the only thing he knew would. To have a woman that strong. His equal.

I know you heard me say I love you on the plane, Jared. Why hadn't he had the courage to tell her? He loved her. Of course he did. He'd been half on his way that night in Nice when he'd learned the truth of her. Fully so after the night she'd given herself to him. And all he'd done since was deny it.

He leaned back and stared at the ceiling. He'd broken Bailey's trust with that clause. The one thing sure to drive her away. And even though he'd had his reasons, they seemed blindingly inappropriate right about now. Not when she was everything he'd never known he wanted.

An idea that might be the product of his jet-lagged brain or pure brilliance, he wasn't sure which, entered his head. He wasn't letting her go. Not a chance.

CHAPTER THIRTEEN

WHEN BAILEY HAD left Las Vegas for California, a freshly minted business degree in her pocket and a lifetime of wisdom garnered from her very real job and her less-than-ideal family background, she'd thought she had it all figured out. Rely on yourself, don't expect too much and keep your eye on the ball, and you'd get where you were going. That mentality, she decided, driving to work the day after that scene with Jared, would have served her well if she'd actually *employed* it with her boss as well as the job. If she hadn't let herself fall in love with a man with a heart of stone. But somewhere along the way, she'd allowed herself to believe, to want far more than her destiny had ever been when it came to him. And suffered the glaring truth of her life-learned rule: wanting more than what you were destined to have was a recipe for heartbreak.

She peeled herself out of her car and walked into her favorite coffee shop in San Jose. Their argument hadn't really been about the clause. It had been about her loving him and being afraid he would never return it.

The lineup of slouchily dressed students, computer nerds and suits was three deep on either side. She chose the typically faster one and tapped her foot impatiently on the faux hardwood floor. Maybe Jared was right, maybe she was running. Maybe it was just easier that way when you wanted what you couldn't have.

The line finally cleared. Christian, the jean-clad, scruffy-looking barista who served her every morning, gave her a curious look as she slid a bill toward him. "Didn't expect to see you here this morning."

"Because this morning is any different from the last five years?" Her attempted humor came out bitter and unattractive. "Sorry," she winced. "Bad morning."

He pushed his funky glasses farther up his nose. "Have you read the paper this morning?"

She shook her head. That was part of her Americano ritual *after* she'd triaged her email. "Why?"

He yelled her order to the barista mixing the drinks. "It's been the talk of the place this morning. You should get on that."

She lifted a brow. "Anything in particular I should be looking for?"

"You'll know it when you see it." He pushed her money back at her. "Drink's on the house, by the way. You look like you need it."

He took the next customer's order. Bailey shook her head, picked up her Americano and drove to work, her re-created resignation burning a hole in her pocket.

Aria called as she was walking through the front doors of the office.

"I gotta admit, even with all his imperfections, *that* would do it for me."

Bailey frowned, using her elbows to negotiate the doors. "What *are* you talking about?"

"Have you read the paper this morning?"

"Why does everyone keep asking me that? What earth-shattering thing has happened? Did Jared make an announcement about Maison?"

"Oh my," Aria sighed. "You really haven't read it. He has certainly made a statement, but it wasn't about Maison."

"Great," Bailey muttered. Another illuminating Jaredism to set the internet ablaze.

"Did you say you have your first executive committee meeting this morning?" Aria asked.

Bailey cradled the phone against her ear and jabbed the call button for the elevator. "I do. If I don't resign first."

"I suggest you read page five of the *Chronicle* before you do that. Then call me. I will kill you if you don't call me."

"Aria." She stepped onto the elevator. "What's going on?"

The iron box swallowed up her call. She hit the button for the twenty-sixth floor, and thought about what Christian had said. *Didn't expect you to be in today…* What did that mean?

She exited the elevator, went straight to the PR department where she collected the *Chronicle* and took it back to her desk. Coffee in hand, she flipped to page five. An open letter from Jared took up the entire page. It was headlined, The Truth about Women—A Rebuttal.

Oh. My. God. He had not. Eyes glued to the page, she started reading.

A few weeks ago, I wrote a manifesto titled "The Truth about Women." Intended as an honest if tongue-in-cheek summary of my views of women both in the boardroom and bedroom, it has provoked a great deal of debate, resonating with some of you and provoking anger in others.

At the time I wrote it I honestly believed everything I said. Experience had taught me that many women do not want the career life we as a society have insisted they do. That cries of a glass ceiling were perpetuated by females caught up in their own self-deception. And if the truth be known, I was not overly sold on a woman's place in the boardroom, nor her ability to stand toe-to-toe with a man.

Then I had the chance to work with a woman I have admired for years, my chief marketing officer, Bailey St. John. In keeping with my theme of nothing but the truth here, I have to admit I severely underestimated her talent. I did not give credit where credit was due. She is not only a superior thinker to any other marketer I have ever had the opportunity to work with, male or female, she could likely wipe the floor with most of them.

This extraordinary woman also taught me something else. Something far more important than the value of a woman in the boardroom. She has proven me wrong about a woman's place in my life. Hers. She has taught me that I can connect with another person on a deeper level, that I do want someone in my life in a forever sense, not just for the sake of the nuclear family, but because I love her. For who she is. For her courage. For what she's taught me. She has made me a better man.

So here is my offer, Bailey, with all my imperfections as previously noted:

I offer you the homestead, and all the baking supplies in it, minus the white picket fence because Pacific Heights does not consider this fashionable.

I offer you a ring and a lifetime commitment.

I offer you a lion in the bedroom because that part is still true and I know you like it. Love it, actually.

And most importantly, if I am lucky enough to have you I am offering you complete honesty—after a mistake I swear I will never make again. Even when it's hard. Even when it hurts because that works for us.

If you're interested in all I have to offer, you know
where to find me.
    All my love,
    Jared

Her eyes blurred as she read the last sentence. Hot tears
spilled down her cheeks in a wet line that dripped into her
Americano. She reread the whole thing. Stared at it hard.
Vaguely registered the arrival of Tate Davidson and the
fact that her executive meeting started in five minutes.

She blew her nose. Fixed her lipstick. Clutched her notebook and letter of resignation to her chest and followed
Tate upstairs to the boardroom. It was packed with a full
contingent of board members as well as executives at the
vice president level and above, presided over by the chairman of the board, Sam Walters.

And Jared. Seated at the head of the table beside Sam,
his gaze, which might be described as distinctly hostile,
was trained on her. As was every set of eyes in the room,
for that matter, and honestly, she could do without that.

Sam waved her and Tate into two chairs at the front.
Bailey sat down, glad for the seat given her knocking
knees. Tate opened the meeting, and began going through
the financials. Jared took off his jacket and loosened his
tie. Started drumming his fingers on the table. Tate announced the Maison deal to much applause, the buzz in
the room palpable. He waited while the other directors
congratulated Jared, then turned to the CEO for a word.

"I'm sorry," Jared said, waving a hand at Tate, his gaze
still pinned on Bailey, "but did you read the paper this
morning?"

Her lips curved, his disheveled appearance, the agitated
air about him, solidifying what she already knew. Jared
Stone was irresistible. "Five minutes ago," she said evenly.
"I was late this morning."

The scowl on his face grew. "You have anything you'd like to share?"

"Yes," she said softly, because you could hear a pin drop in the room, it was that quiet. "But I'd prefer to do it in private."

He sat back, blue eyes stormy. Julie Walcott, his VP of PR, raised her hand. "Can I make a request? Can we make this the last manifesto? It's such a work of art we should allow it to become infamous."

"Considering this one just about killed me," Jared growled, "that would be a definitive yes."

Sam took control of the meeting after that. Somewhere near the end, she found herself the bewildered owner of a whole new set of responsibilities Jared bestowed on her in a bid to go back to doing what he did best. He relinquished the "first look" privileges he had over Stone Industries' marketing and handed them to her. From now on everyone on the PR, advertising and marketing teams would report to her. He did not, Jared stressed, want to spend his time approving ad campaigns.

She stared shocked at him while Tate Davidson nearly lost his breakfast. It was a controversial call, no doubt, but given the stormy nature of her boss at the moment, no one was saying a word.

Lunchtime arrived. She stood up with everyone else, snatching her resignation off the table. Jared appeared at her elbow. "My office," he growled and propelled her down the hall into his minimalistic haven. Bailey stood, paper clutched in her hands, as he shut the door and leaned against it, his stance turning predatory.

"What *is* that in your hands?"

"My resignation."

His gaze narrowed. "You aren't resigning. I feel a sense of déjà vu here."

She drank him in, the same fierce warrior in evidence

as the one in her bedroom that night in Nice when he'd promised to back her no matter what.

"Did you mean everything you said in that rebuttal?"

He nodded. "Every word. Including the part where I declared my love for you in a national newspaper."

Her heart melted, so full of emotion she didn't know where to start. "Promises aren't in your DNA."

"I didn't think love was in my DNA either," he countered roughly, snagging her sleeve and tugging her closer. "And now look at me."

She was. He was everything she'd never dreamed she could have. And so much more.

"Seeing my father threw me. I needed time to process. To understand my feelings. But never for one minute did I change my mind about you. About what I said on the plane." He ran his thumb across her cheek. "I will always tell you the truth, even when you don't want to hear it."

"I know," she whispered. "I just needed to hear you say it. Write it. Whatever. Actually can you say it?"

He lowered his head to hers. "I love you. I've loved you from that night in Nice."

He kissed her then, slow and deep. She was ready to sink into it completely, into *him* completely, when he set her away from him with a determined movement.

"Hey," she protested. "That wasn't—"

The words died in her throat as he pulled a jeweler's box from his inside pocket. "You weren't supposed to be late this morning. I was going to give you this."

Her heart jumped into her mouth as he flipped the box open. Nestled inside the blue jeweler's box sat a diamond eternity band that sparkled in the light. "You can have another if you like," he said huskily, "you can have ten. But this is my promise to be your constant, Bailey St. John. Marry me."

She shoved her hand at him. He slipped the ring on.

The diamonds, hugging her finger in an unending circle of fire, made her heart take flight.

He brought her hand to his lips. "Is that a yes?"

"Yes."

"Good. After this meeting, I'm taking you home to celebrate."

"After?" she pouted.

"I just gave you direct responsibility for all marketing activity. You'd better take the helm while you can."

"True," she murmured. "I do love you, Jared Stone. I'm not afraid to say it."

His gaze darkened. "You can tell me that again tonight. Over and over."

She did. Many times as he proved his nickname All-Night Jared Stone was aptly earned. The ring sparkling on her finger made that just fine with her. He was hers; he would always be hers, she knew that. And in his arms, Bailey finally found herself. Not the old Bailey, not the new Bailey, just the Bailey she was destined to be.

* * * * *

MILLS & BOON®

Why not subscribe?
Never miss a title and save money too!

Here's what's available to you if you join the
exclusive **Mills & Boon Book Club** today:

✦ *Titles up to a month ahead of the shops*
✦ *Amazing discounts*
✦ *Free P&P*
✦ *Earn Bonus Book points that can be redeemed
   against other titles and gifts*
✦ *Choose from monthly or pre-paid plans*

Still want more?
Well, if you join today we'll even give you
50% OFF your first parcel!

So visit **www.millsandboon.co.uk/subs**
or call Customer Relations on 020 8288 2888
to be a part of this exclusive Book Club!

14_ST_7

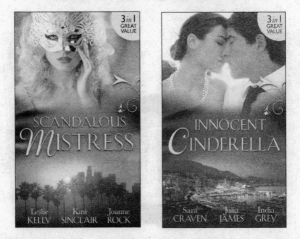